"My stalker's back, Cruse." Bayley shuddered. **"He's been in my house. When I got home, I found a rose on my kitchen table. With a note."**

She retreated to the swing on her porch. Up until now, she'd felt in control. She wouldn't let some sick man take that from her.

Cruse crouched in front of her and placed a warm hand on her knee. "My partner's on his way. He'll help find out where the flower and note came from."

"I'm strong. I can handle a lot," she said. "But I don't know if I can go through this again."

He gathered her into his very strong arms.

Bayley should be wary of him. She didn't want to depend on anyone but God for strength. Especially not this man. He was a cop, another protector like the many men who had guarded her over the years.

So why did she still cling to Cruse?

Because she realized that the terror hadn't ended. It was just the beginning.

STEPHANIE NEWTON

penned her first suspense story—complete with illustrations—at the age of twelve, but didn't write seriously until her youngest child was in first grade. She lives in Northwest Florida where she gains inspiration from the sugar-white sand, aqua-blue-green water of the Gulf of Mexico and the many unusual and interesting things you see when you live on the beach. You can find her most often enjoying the water with her family, or at their church, where her husband is the pastor. Visit Stephanie at her Web site, www.stephanienewton.net or send an e-mail to newtonwriter@gmail.com.

PERFECT TARGET

STEPHANIE NEWTON

Steeple
Hill®

Published by Steeple Hill Books™

STEEPLE HILL BOOKS

Steeple
Hill®

Recycling programs
for this product may
not exist in your area.

ISBN-13: 978-0-373-44332-1
ISBN-10:   0-373-44332-3

PERFECT TARGET

Printed in U.S.A.

The Lord is my light and my salvation; Whom shall
I fear? The Lord is the stronghold of my life;
Of whom shall I be afraid?
—*Psalms* 27:1

For Allen, who never stopped believing, and for my children, God's amazing gifts—you never cease to amaze me.

So many people helped in the crafting of this book. My unbelievably supportive critique partners and friends Brenda Minton and Holly LaPat, you've been here since the beginning and I'm so thankful for you. Mentor and sweet friend Catherine Mann, I have been so blessed by your friendship and the gift of your time and talent!

Thanks to my fabulous agent, Barbara Collins Rosenberg, who read this book umpteen times and took a chance on me.

To Melissa Endlich, my talented editor—thanks for seeing the possibilities. I'm so thrilled to be working with you!

A special thanks to former firefighter and youth minister T.J. Emma, Midway Fire Commission Chair Jacque Gorris, and to Tony Hughes for helping Cruse figure out how to rescue Bayley. Thanks to Karen Clark for the surfing lessons.

To the real policemen and women and to the men and women who give their lives helping others in real, hands-on ministry like Hope House—I am in awe of you and so, so thankful that you do what you do.

ONE

Bayley Foster held a dead man in her arms.

And tried as hard as she could *not* to think about it. Mostly it took all her concentration to keep swimming for shore. Hoping with all her heart that her neighbor heard her screams as she'd launched herself off the deck of her beach house. Late afternoon, he should be home.

Bayley'd thought the floating man might still be alive when she'd seen the dark head bobbing in the water in the late afternoon sun. Seeing him up close, she knew he was dead. He looked dead. More than that, his soul was gone.

Still, he was a person, someone's dad or brother or friend. He deserved better than drifting to some unknown watery grave in the Gulf of Mexico. His family deserved to know what happened to him.

She could easily imagine her family in that situation, never knowing what happened to her if her stalker hadn't been stopped.

She didn't want to touch the body, stifled a gag even now just gripping the collar of his suit coat to drag him behind her toward shore. But she was making it—one awkward, frog-legged stroke at a time.

Just her and the dead guy.

Maybe she should call him Bob. Or not. He kind of looked

like Great-uncle Harold. Since Harold was dead, too, surely he wouldn't mind sharing his name for a while.

The riptide caught her by surprise, grabbed her in its iron grip, drawing her away from where she wanted to go. Shore. Safety.

The current sucked at her legs, every stroke like pulling through mud, the body dragging behind her. For the first time, she realized how stupid it had been for her to go in after him. She'd heard the stories of well-meaning tourists who didn't know better facing the vicious undertow, trying to save someone else when they couldn't even save themselves. She was a local—a Florida native—she should know better.

Where was her neighbor? What she wouldn't give to see him come swishing by on his surfboard about now. A retired cop two doors down—over the past few months, she'd come to trust his dear face, horn-rimmed glasses and all. She knew he wouldn't let her down.

She was so tired already. Giving her head a shake, Bayley cleared the clammy, salt-soaked hair from her eyes. She commanded herself to pay attention to her surroundings and forced her muscles to continue the strokes parallel to the beach that would deliver her from the riptide.

She wanted to rest, but that was dangerous—she'd only get sucked out farther. *Keep swimming.* Her leg muscles burned, each halfhearted kick shooting shards of pain up to her hips. But she couldn't stop. Wouldn't stop.

"Just a little rest. That wouldn't hurt, would it, Harold?" Yeah, it would hurt. If she gave in, she might end up taking her eternal rest, just like Harold. Fighting against that siren's voice in her head, she kept kicking, slowing against her will.

Focus on the task, Bayley. She was taking him home, this man whom somebody loved. Wouldn't she have wanted someone to do the same for her? The nearly healed muscle in her right shoulder where she'd been stabbed screamed at her, reminding her of how close she'd come to being dead. Like this guy.

But God had been faithful, even then, when He'd felt so far away. He'd brought her through circumstances that made her shudder to think about. He had plans for her. She knew He did, and He would bring her through this, too.

She struggled to keep her head above the water. Salty waves poured into her mouth with every gasp. At least it would be fast.

How could she even think that? She'd spent the past four years of her life fighting for survival. With God's help, she'd won against a determined stalker. She *refused* to die here when she had the strength to fight.

"Come on, Harold." Kicking harder, she inched forward.

The riptide spit her out as suddenly and effortlessly as it had gripped her. Bayley drifted for a few seconds in the normal ebb and flow of the surf, able—finally—to swim toward the shore. She looked up to gauge the distance and saw the roofline of her house, and her friendly cop's, and Mrs. P's. The other colorful homes on wooden stilt pilings along the Florida Panhandle shore.

And…that guy so wasn't *her* cop coming to rescue her.

He plowed through the surf, looking like a blond Adonis, already waist deep, his black Sea Breeze PD T-shirt wet from the waves slapping his broad chest.

Her feet hit the sand. She struggled forward, groping with her toes for purchase in the churning water. A huge breaker knocked into her and she went down, tumbling. Her knee scraped against the sand, the force tearing her skin, leaving it raw and stinging in the salt water.

A hand grasped her T-shirt and hauled her up and out of the water. Impervious to the force of the waves, he set her on her feet and held her there.

"Are you okay?" His green eyes, nearly the exact color of the ocean, filled with concern.

"I think so, but this guy's not."

The guy got his first look at the body, and shot her a somber glance. "He's dead."

"I know." Bayley wanted to explain she wasn't really that clueless, but she didn't have the energy—or the breath—to try. It was all she could do to keep putting one foot in front of the other with the waves beating against her back.

"You can let go of him."

She still had the fabric of the man's suit coat twisted in her fist. Looking at it, she barely recognized her own fingers, white and wrinkled from the water.

The stranger's hand grasped her elbow. "You can let go of him now. I'll take care of him."

Somehow, she knew he would. She opened her fingers, wincing against the cramp from being clutched too long in the same position. "Rest in peace, Harold."

"Get out of the water, now." The cop lifted the man into his arms without even a grunt of effort. He surged out of the ocean.

Bayley stumbled into the shallow foam at the edge of the Gulf, red and blue lights sending long weird beams from the road out over the uneven sand. Two paramedics pounded across the dunes, a stretcher between them.

She sank to her knees and rolled onto her back, the surf breaking just beyond her feet and sliding over her legs. Boneless, her body melted into the sand beneath her, her eyes closing in relief. She could hear the officer's deep voice directing the scene, so firm and in control.

Just like a cop, always having to be in charge. She drifted a little further toward sleep. Too bad, 'cause he had really pretty green eyes.

Cruse Conyers handed the body off to the paramedics, but probably not for long. Unnatural, unexplained deaths were investigated by detectives. So he'd be spending some more time with Bayley Foster's "Harold."

Yeah, he knew who his neighbor was. Anyone with a newspaper would. And he knew that her family owned the house two doors down, though he had few memories of her there over the years.

She'd been incredibly lucky to get out of the water on a red flag day like today. Only the very stupid or very brave would have done what she did. He didn't know her personally, but the retired cop who'd borrowed his house while he'd been undercover for the past two months had raved about her. She wasn't stupid.

Brave, then. His sister wouldn't have gotten within ten feet of a dead body, much less attached herself to him like Velcro and dragged him out of the ocean.

Cruse scanned the crowd of onlookers, all gawking at the dead man. Where was Bayley?

She'd followed him out of the water. Hadn't she?

He spun around, taking a step back toward the ocean. Dusk was falling, dappling the sand with shadows. But he saw her, a dark figure, lying half in the water, half out.

He broke into a jog. Had he missed something? She'd been tired, exhausted even, but…maybe she had a head injury and he hadn't given her the chance to tell him, or maybe she'd hurt her neck in that tumble she took in the surf.

Reaching her side, he stopped. Her eyes were closed, but her chest rose and fell. Sharp, quick breaths still. He didn't move her, not yet. If she had a neck injury, he'd only hurt her.

He touched her shoulder, careful not to shake her.

Dark blue eyes flashed open, zeroing in on his with quick comprehension. A flicker of pain crossed her face as she struggled to sit. He stood, ready to whistle for the paramedics. The dead guy could wait. His injuries certainly couldn't get any worse.

"Wait, I'm just beat."

She laid her head down on her knees, her dark brown hair covering her face. Now that her legs were out of the water, he could see blood coursing from her knee down her shin. She *was* hurt. And though it was far from chilly, the summer heat was fading. After the exertion of swimming, she'd be cooling down, and fast.

She'd hauled a dead man out of the water, swimming against a riptide. Somebody should help her. He leaned down and scooped her up in his arms. She yelped.

"Be still. You're exhausted and you need to get inside and get out of those wet clothes." He grinned down at her. "And since we haven't been introduced, I'm Cruse Conyers."

"Bayley Foster. And my legs work fine." Navy-blue eyes snapped.

"Relax, door-to-door delivery is part of the service."

She shook her head like a teacher with an incorrigible child, and his smile faded away.

Cop. Job. Dead guy. He tried to focus on that—anything to get his mind off the fact that his arms were full of soft, curvy Bayley. Where she rested against his chest was far from cold. Bayley wasn't the kind of girl Cruse had those thoughts about. She was a nice girl, a home-and-family kind of girl. And while he once might have dreamed of that kind of life, he knew now it was out of the question for him.

He'd nailed the lid on those dreams with the same nails that had hung his police academy diploma on the wall, joining the force in hopes of fixing the unfixable.

His little sister had been attacked, the criminal having taken everything from her but her life. He couldn't change the past for his sister. The best he could do for her was to save some other poor woman from the same fate.

Mrs. Phillips, the next-door neighbor on the other side of Bayley, had caught sight of them and beelined toward him.

Her short, black hair frizzed in the humid evening air and flapped up and down as she slogged through the fine sand.

"Cruse. Oh, Cruse? Is that Bayley? Is she okay?"

"I'm fine, Mrs. P, just tired." Bayley squirmed into a semi-upright position, which to her probably seemed like a good idea.

His gut clenched, his fingers tightening involuntarily to curve around her ribs. Old temptations, the kind he used to follow without a second thought, threatened to overwhelm him. He hadn't been a Christian long, but he knew he wasn't that guy, not anymore.

Think about boring things, Cruse. Writing reports, flossing his teeth, uh, folding clothes—not that he ever did that. Oh, and those decorating shows his sister liked to watch. Those were really boring. Shaved trees, shaped like pelicans. *Topiary, topiary, topiary.*

His mental chant wasn't working. She was going to have to walk. He set her on her feet and grabbed her hand, pulling her toward her beach house.

"You've got to be upset, dear. I mean, after all, you were swimming with a dead man." Mrs. P fluttered up the steps and followed them through the half-open door into Bayley's kitchen.

Cruse needed to get out of Bayley's house and fast. He was her neighbor, and a cop. He could watch out for her, protect her, help her with heavy boxes. What he couldn't do was think about her in *that* way.

Pulling a chair from the table with his foot, Cruse pushed Bayley gently down. She shivered in the air-conditioning.

Cruse strode into the bedroom, snatching up the first thing he saw—a warm, worn quilt from the bottom of Bayley's bed. Back in the kitchen, he wrapped her from head to toe, wooden dining chair included.

Mrs. P bustled in Bayley's all-white kitchen, heating a

kettle, two ceramic mugs on the counter with tea-bag tags hanging out. The self-appointed neighborhood grandmother had things under control here. Bayley didn't need him and that suited him just fine. She'd needed help and he'd helped her. That's what he did. He helped people. He protected. *He didn't get involved.*

"Get some rest, Bayley. I've got to get back outside to the scene, but I'll have some questions for you later." He nodded at the diminutive older lady, now patting Bayley's back as she bobbed her head at him. "Mrs. P. Take care."

Outside, the freedom and wildness of the Gulf balanced him as he took a deep breath of the humid air. He'd chosen this place because of the vastness of the ocean. It had enough space for him.

Taking the stairs down two at a time, he met his partner, Slayton Cross, coming up. "Details, Slay. Go."

Slayton took his PalmPilot out of his shirt pocket and turned it on, but didn't glance at it. "There's no ID. Lividity indicates he was killed somewhere else. Ligature marks on his wrists. In my opinion, it's definitely a homicide."

They stepped off the stairs into the sand, and lingered, Slayton leaning back on the banister, one foot on the bottom step, his fingers beating a familiar tattoo. After two years of being his partner, Cruse could almost tune it out. Almost.

"We lucked out. Another two days in the water and he'd have been as useless as the body that washed in a couple of days ago. At least we can get fingerprints off this guy. If he's in the system we'll ID him."

A few straggling onlookers remained, but most had left the crime scene unit—CSU—to their job gathering evidence, though there'd probably be little left to find after hours in the ocean. "You follow up with the CSU. I'll get a statement from Bayley."

"Bayley?" Slayton's fingers went back to tapping on the rail.

"My neighbor. The woman who rescued our floater?"

"Got it." Slayton tucked his notebook away. "See you tomorrow."

Night had fallen. The beach was dark, the ocean a vast, black backdrop behind them. The CSU had set up generator-run floodlights, punctuated by the flash of their cameras documenting the scene. The photos would be of limited value considering the victim hadn't been killed here.

Cruse circled the area. He wouldn't leap to conclusions, but fully dressed men, in suits, no less, didn't usually wash up here. Likely, the two murders were connected.

He glanced up the beach to Bayley's light-blue-painted beach house. She'd be inside, having her cup of tea with Mrs. Phillips. Maybe she would have put some music on to relax after a difficult day. He didn't know much about her, but he knew he didn't belong there.

He had a house in this neighborhood—a small one—but he'd bought two lots here ten years ago. He'd lived in a trailer on one and eaten peanut butter for three years in order to pay for them. And he'd done well with his investment. He'd sold the extra million-dollar lot to build his house and had made enough to support his sister when she'd needed him. But he sure didn't fit in with the vacation crowd that summered here—the silver-spoon crowd that had always been too good for him, no matter that his portfolio now matched theirs.

He turned back to the murder victim. This was Cruse's place. The crime scene. Not that insular world up there that Bayley called home. And it would be best for him to remember that.

"You're going to die."

Bayley reared her hand back to pitch the phone across the room, the voice of her worst nightmare still echoing in her ear. Just in time, she checked herself. And she kept the phone to her ear, managed the fear, knowing he couldn't hurt her anymore.

He couldn't touch her physically and he couldn't steal her God-given peace of mind. This man who'd stalked her, nearly stolen her life, was in jail. Securely behind bars. She took a deep breath and blew out the rest of her anxiety.

"Yep. It's the circle of life. We're all born and we all die. Have a nice day." She slammed the phone down.

Tomorrow she'd report the call and he'd have his phone privileges revoked—again. Picking up the stereo remote, she un-muted Aretha. *R-E-S-P-E-C-T.*

Bayley'd been finding out what respect meant for her. How could she teach self-respect at the women's shelter where she worked if she didn't walk the talk herself? She couldn't pray with those women, tell them to trust God and themselves, if she wasn't doing the same. Every day she learned more, and it was a journey.

She was alive. She didn't take it for granted, not one bit of it. She was determined to have a normal life. Even today. Especially today.

Two hours ago, she'd finally convinced sweet Mrs. P to go home. By the time Bayley'd gotten out of the shower, all of the flashing lights, all of the police and the hoopla had been gone with the heat of the day.

Now she would conquer another of her fears. *Dinner.* On her front porch, she reached into her pocket for the matches and turned the gas on under the grill. She lit a match, closed her eyes and flipped it. When she didn't hear the burners light, she squinted one eye open and groaned. The match had landed on the grate and gone out in the wind blowing off the Gulf.

"I'm a grown woman," she muttered to herself. "I can light a barbecue grill."

Pep talk…check. Matches…check. Bayley struck it, tossed

it and jumped back three feet as the burners whooshed and flames shot out of the grill.

Yikes. Okay, not pretty, but since she didn't set the deck on fire, she'd count it as a success.

She padded barefoot into the house for the meat, a defiant swing in her step from the music drifting through the back door's screen. Juggling the plate with her marinated steak, the tongs and the salt and pepper grinders, she started for the door.

The phone jangled behind her.

Bayley stopped midstep, her heart stalling, then skipping ahead. It wouldn't be him again. It wasn't like he could get to the phone whenever he wanted to.

She backtracked through the kitchen, set the plate down and glanced at the caller ID. Mrs. P. The woman needed someone to mother. Maybe Bayley should get her a kitten. "Hello?"

"Oh, Bayley, I'm so glad I got you on the phone." Her words tumbled, one over the other. "I just called 911. I saw someone *lurking* under your house."

Bayley shot a glance at the back door, standing wide-open. Fear exploded through her—no wimpy feeling of trepidation this time—but full-blown, paralyzing fear.

You're going to die, he'd said.

She forced her voice to work, trying for level and calm, not quite succeeding. "What exactly did you see, Mrs. P?"

"I only caught a glimpse, but I saw a shadowy figure sneaking around the pilings."

Acting a composure she didn't feel, Bayley said, "Thanks for telling me, sweetie. I'll let you know when the police get here."

She hung up the phone, and battled the desire to run and slam the door. If anyone had reason to fear danger in life, danger even from perfect strangers, Bayley did. But she would not hide trembling in a closet. Been there, done that, as the saying went.

Bayley strode across the room to her purse and pulled out her gun, a little Glock that a former bodyguard had taught her to use. She was more than proficient with it. She was really, really good.

Her victim days were behind her.

She closed the outside door, silently sliding the bolt home, the music from the house now over-loud as she listened for noises that didn't fit in the sultry coastal night. The cops had been called—she needed to get to a safe place, get ready and wait.

She slipped down the hall, not turning on lights as she knew the way by heart. When she reached the bedroom at the end of the hall, she stopped. She'd be able to see anyone coming down the hall silhouetted in the light from the living room, but he wouldn't be able to see her.

She stretched out to lie prone on the floor. Her bodyguards had taught her that in this situation, her chances were better on the ground than presenting a larger vertical target. An intruder wouldn't think to look down, giving her the advantage.

Her heartbeat thudding in her ears, she waited. Gritty sand she'd missed sweeping dug into her elbows, but she didn't shift away from it. She'd been afraid so many times, so many nights. She could make it through this. A few minutes and the cops would be here.

Bayley lay in the dark, every noise a new chance for her imagination to work overtime, even the creaking and popping from the summer-heated roof as it cooled. She exhaled. *Remain calm,* the most important instruction from her teachers.

Footsteps pounded up her outside steps. Her stomach clenched as she got ready for whatever—whoever—might come through that door.

Knocking. And a voice. "Sea Breeze PD. Bayley, it's Cruse Conyers. Can you open the door, please?"

Bayley relaxed, letting her forehead drop onto her out-stretched arms.

She scrambled to her feet, lifting the edge of her tank top and settling the gun at the small of her back. At the door she looked through the peephole. Cruse Conyers. In plain clothes, his badge and gun obvious on his hip, Cruse wasn't in full warrior mode—she could tell that from experience—but it was close.

No doubt he was sexy in his tame-the-world kind of way, but he was another protector. And she'd had more than enough of that kind of man—no matter how cute he was with that blond surfer hair.

As she opened the door, he narrowed his eyes. "Bayley?"

She stuck out a hand. "Hey, Cruse. I didn't expect to see you again so soon."

He took her hand, but held it loosely, not shaking it, studying her face. "Did you call the police about a prowler?"

"No, Mrs. P did. She thought she saw someone sneaking around under the house, but I didn't see anything."

His fingers tightened on hers, and he pulled her slightly closer. "She told you there was an intruder and you went outside to check it out?"

Bayley withdrew her hand firmly and tucked it under her other arm. "No. I stayed up here and waited for the police to come. I'm not stupid, or helpless."

"Didn't think you were," he said easily. "Why don't we take a look around? Make sure there's nothing out of order down there?"

Not even slightly mollified, Bayley followed Cruse down the stairs and as he walked the edge of the concrete flooring under the house. All of the houses on this beach resembled hers, built on wooden stilts with a concrete floor carport or patio area underneath. "I thought you were off duty after the…incident today."

"I am." He clicked on the big silver flashlight he carried and played it across the surrounding sand. "You live two doors down from me. Even if I didn't have a scanner—which I do—someone would have called me. Looks like there are footprints in the sand around the edge of the concrete. Did you make these?"

Footprints. Maybe there had been an intruder. Bayley had been operating on the theory that Mrs. P was a little imaginative, but if there really was a prowler... Bayley's stomach lurched.

"Bayley?"

She jumped at the sound of Cruse's voice. "It's hard to tell, the sand's so soft there. I don't think I made those, but it's been a while since we've had rain. It could have been anyone."

Cruse paced off the rest of the concrete and tested the lock on the storage room. "You're right. It could even have been the people around this afternoon. I don't see any sign of a trespasser. To be safe, though, I'd keep the door locked and an eye open."

Just like that, the fear rolled back in, as inevitable as the tide, and made her shake. She had to get a hold of herself. It was nothing. *It had to be nothing.*

"You okay?" Cruse's eyes, deep green tonight, held concern and a touch of wariness.

She forced a smile. "Sure. I'm fine, just a little tired. It was a long afternoon out there today. And I guess I got a little adrenaline rush when my neighbor called."

"There she is now."

Bayley looked toward her neighbor's house. The diminutive Mrs. P, dyed-black hair standing at attention in the wind, hovered at her back door. She might have been pretending she wasn't nosy, but if so, she wasn't doing a very good job.

Bayley smiled.

"I'll walk you up and then I'll need to ask your neighbor a few questions about what she saw."

"That's not necessary."

"I need to hear what she saw."

"I know that. I mean you don't have to walk me up."

One corner of Cruse's mouth kicked up in a half smile. "I know."

Bayley rolled her eyes and crossed to the stairs, Cruse behind her. As she started up, she felt more than saw him lean on the newel-post at the base of the stairs.

She was almost at the top when she heard him say, "You got a permit for that thing?"

She stopped in her tracks.

He laughed softly, and she turned around to glare at him. "As a matter of fact, I do. Wanna see it?"

She raised one eyebrow at him, and another soft laugh made her wish she had something to throw at him.

"Not this time. If you've got some time in the morning, though, I'd like to get a statement about what happened today."

"I don't know anything."

"That's what I figured. I just need your statement for the record."

"For the record, what happened to the cop neighbor that I *liked?*"

He laughed again and pushed off the banister toward her neighbor's house. "Don't forget to lock up, now."

She had the best locks money could buy. She could lock her house. Too bad she couldn't lock out the fear as easily.

TWO

Cruse woke at dawn for his workout—*woke* being a relative term. He hadn't slept much. He'd gotten up every couple of hours to make a trek outside, walking around Bayley Foster's property, wishing he didn't care, wondering why he did. What would she have thought if she'd seen him? Probably that he was the crazy person that Mrs. P had seen lurking under Bayley's house.

He needed to work off some restless energy in a serious way. Normally a run on the beach would do it, but… He clicked on the weather, the crash of the waves outside his house already telling him what he wanted to know. Oh, yeah.

Surf was up.

He slid his feet into flip flops and walked out on his deck to study the scene. The waves were noisy, but that didn't mean they were rideable. Sometimes there was too much chop, or the currents were too strong. But not today.

Cruse took his surfboard from its standard position over his fireplace and began waxing it as he searched for the best place to paddle out. The sand gleamed white against the sometimes emerald, sometimes turquoise green of the water. Sets of three or four awesome waves rolled in from the horizon.

When he couldn't stand it another second, he popped the

wax into his back pocket and took off for the water. A mad dash, and he leaped into the dance. Becoming one with his surfboard, he soared over the first wall of white water. Man, he loved this ocean.

A duck dive carried him through the next wave. The deadly rip current that Bayley battled yesterday was a surfer's dream. Farther out now, he could paddle up the face of the swell and ride it down. When he reached the outside, where the waves were rolling but not breaking, he rested.

For Cruse, this moment sang of freedom. Out here in this immense body of water, he could breathe. He could forget the rotten circumstances he grew up in. Sometimes he could even forget that he'd failed his baby sister so badly.

Here he could narrow his life down to a single focus. Ride the wave. No case, no victim, no pain-filled little-sister eyes. He could almost forget a woman he needed to steer clear of.

He saw it coming—his wave, the second in the set—and he started paddling, getting ready for the takeoff. On his feet, he dropped in along the face. The wind blew his hair, the roar of the water deafening as he simply…flew.

In a few moments this wave would be gone in a flash of spray on the sand, but here and now, in *this* moment, he owned it.

Close to shore, he dropped and rode into the shallows. He would gladly stay until his arms were rubber and his feet numb, but real life called. His partner waited on the beach.

Cruse slung his wet hair off his forehead and, tucking his board under his arm, walked up the sand to Slayton, who'd obviously borrowed a beach chair from Cruse's house. He had his shirt off, face turned to the early morning sun.

"Better watch out—you might get a sunburn." Cruse flicked water on Slayton, who jerked to his feet with a yelp.

"Not likely." Slayton nodded toward Cruse's board. "Great morning for that."

"Perfect. What's up?"

Slayton got to his feet and picked up the chair, flipping his freshly pressed oxford shirt over his shoulder and starting toward Cruse's house. "We've got ID on the floater. His name was Brad Paxton. He was a lawyer here in town, seemingly legit. But he filed a bunch of lawsuits for Save Our Shores."

"Nice clients." The S.O.S. group tended to be more like ecoterrorists than real environmental lobbyists, using scare tactics to make their point. He'd seen the police reports.

"Yeah. That's not the only thing. His wife had called the cops on three different occasions—domestic violence reports—but she never pressed charges."

"So she's a suspect unless we find out different from the autopsy." Cruse stopped at the bottom of the stairs that led up to his deck, turning on the outdoor shower to rinse the salt water and sand off.

"That would be a yes."

He wrapped a towel around his waist and dripped up the stairs, thinking for at least the hundredth time he should really finish painting his house. He'd chosen a slate gray and gotten halfway around on his one-week vacation. The next week, embroiled in a drug-running case, he'd put the brushes in the freezer and planned to get them out on the weekend. That was four months ago.

Slayton followed Cruse into the house, buttoning his shirt. He helped himself to a cup of coffee in Cruse's favorite mug. "You talk to the girl yet?"

"What girl?" He pretended ignorance.

"The one that pulled the floater out."

The image of Bayley last night, in her baby-pink tank top and cutoffs, came to Cruse's mind. But what he remembered most was not the way she looked, but the way she'd tried to hide her fear. "No, that's first on my list this morning, though."

"You get to that. I'll pay a visit to the widow."

"You'll need a warrant for the house."

"Maybe she'll invite me in."

Cruse shot Slayton a "keep dreaming" look. "Call the judge for the warrant."

"Already done."

"Get out of here."

"No, really, I already called Judge Santos."

"No, I mean get out of here. I need to get to work. You're showing me up." Cruse nipped his mug out of Slayton's hand at the last second, darting one last longing look at the surf outside his house as he shoved Slayton out the door. But he had priorities.

Like murder. And a pretty neighbor who seemed to be in trouble. Even though he hadn't told Bayley, he'd been pretty sure someone had been under her house last night. What he didn't know was why.

Bayley sliced through the log of cinnamon and dough that she'd rolled, placing the slices carefully on a cookie sheet. In half an hour, she'd know if she'd made a colossal mess. They looked right, but it was her first try.

She hadn't done so well with the grilling experiment last night. After Cruse left, she'd come upstairs to find the grill dark and cold, out of gas. Later today, she would figure out how to refill it and she would try again.

She was determined to make a life for herself. A real life. An independent life. And not independent with a household staff, either. On her own. Self-sufficient. After four years of being watched every second, she didn't even want a maid in her space. She could clean up after her own self, thank you very much.

Bayley had been viciously attacked, very nearly killed. She didn't hide from life now. She *savored* every blessed moment.

She opened the oven door and slid the rolls in.

"Knock, knock."

"Thomas!" Bayley squealed as she wrenched open the screen door and wrapped her best friend of a bajillion years in a hug. "When your dad was out here last week, he said you'd be in Europe another month."

"You know I can't stay away from the beach that long. And when I found out you were staying here, not just for a vacation…well, that gave me some extra incentive to get home quicker. So you got some coffee for me?"

Bayley took another cup from the cabinet and poured the hot, seriously strong brew for her neighbor. "Did you have any doubt?"

"Pretty safe bet, wasn't it?" Thomas smiled at her, but it didn't reach his eyes. A lock of his light brown hair fell over his forehead and he pushed it back with an impatient motion, reminding her of the five-year-old she'd befriended in kindergarten.

Not one to beat around the bush, especially when she didn't have to, Bayley asked, "What's going on with you? Why are you really back here so early?"

Thomas hesitated. "Things aren't going well at the job site. There are some things I need to handle personally. At least, according to my dad."

She groaned. "When is he going to realize that you weren't made for the construction business?"

"When he gets tired of footing the bills for my mistakes, I guess." A fleeting half smile crossed his face. "He's given me enough chances. It's not his fault I can't be like Charlie."

Her friend needed confidence desperately—something Bayley couldn't give him. She was still learning that one herself, finding who she was in God. One thing she did know—faith wasn't transferable. She couldn't share hers with Thomas, but she could give him a little reassurance. "Who knows what your brother would have been if he'd lived? He wasn't perfect and wouldn't be perfect now. You're so gifted in other ways. Your father is the one missing out if he doesn't realize it."

Cup in hand, she strolled to the fireplace, studying the painting over the mantel. The bold slashes of color rolled and spread across the canvas in a glorious abstract view of ocean and sky. "This has always been my favorite of yours. It's so incredibly powerful."

He came up behind her and threw an arm around her neck and shoulders like the brother he very nearly was. "Could you be any more prejudiced?"

"Maybe not." She laughed with Thomas, who—finally—had a genuine smile on his face.

His cell phone buzzed and the peaceful, pleased look she'd worked so hard to put on his face vanished. He squinted at the caller ID readout. "Business calls."

He paused for a moment, his brow creased. "Listen, you be careful. Take care of yourself, okay?"

She looked at him sharply—had he already heard about the rescue yesterday?—but he kissed her cheek and slid out the door, his head bent in concentration over the phone. With a heavy heart, she watched as he disappeared down the stairs. He'd never been particularly strong. When they were seven, she punched the class bully for calling Thomas a fathead. She couldn't help but think he needed someone to stick up for him now.

She hadn't heard Thomas's soft footfalls as he went down the stairs, but she heard someone coming up now. She stepped back from the door. Not that there was any place to hide.

Cruse stuck his head around the corner and knocked on the wall as he came around. "Bayley? It's Cruse Conyers."

Great. Bayley tightened the tie of her lavender chenille robe and stepped to the door. "Hey, Cruse."

Cruse sniffed. "What's that smell?"

"Coffee and— Oh, no!" She ran for the kitchen. "Come on in."

She snatched a dish towel off the counter and threw open the oven. The rolls were on the dark side of golden brown—but at least she hadn't charred them. She set them on the stove, and turned to find Cruse watching her, an amused look on his face.

She couldn't help it. She got defensive. "What?"

"Nothing. They look great." He paused. "I haven't eaten."

"You want a roll? Really?"

"Yes, really. Do you have icing?"

His hopeful expression did her in. Who woulda thunk big macho Cruse had a sweet tooth? Bayley went to the fridge and got the little bowl of glaze she'd made earlier and handed it to Cruse, who stared at it as if he'd never seen anything like it before.

"You made this from scratch? Those rolls didn't come out of a tube?"

Bayley pulled the tie on her robe a little tighter, this whole domestic scene getting just a little too intimate for comfort. She smacked a spatula on top of the bowl. "Get busy. I've got to get dressed or I'm going to be late for work."

Cruse stared at the spreader. Bayley Foster had managed to surprise him again. He thought he'd had her nailed as the prima-donna spoiled princess, an image he'd formed years ago from a brief glance of her when he was a beat cop and she was a college girl—she must have been a sophomore or freshman. She'd had all her friends out to the beach house.

He'd been living in his beat-up, fifth-hand trailer. She and her friends hadn't spared him a second look. Neither had her family, for that matter. Though her father had a word with him about how embarrassing it was for the neighbors to have that trailer in the neighborhood. Years later, the old man didn't like his half-painted house any better.

Later he'd heard about the mess with the stalker. How could he not? Even if he hadn't heard about it as a cop on the force, he'd have heard about it on the news. Her father's ill-advised way of handling it dragged the media into it rather than protecting her privacy. She had to have felt violated on every side, something he hadn't considered as a younger cop.

Cruse dug the spatula into the bowl of frosting and slapped it on one of the rolls. He didn't think their opinion had bothered him then, but apparently it made an impression. He certainly had one of Bayley as the born-with-a-silver-spoon-in-her-mouth heiress, but she hadn't acted like one when she dragged a dead guy out of the ocean.

Cruse opened cabinet doors until he found the plates, took two down and slid the rolls from pan to plate.

He heard her heels tap-tapping across the tile floor in the hall. She may have looked vulnerable and unpretentious last night, but she looked the rich-princess part today. Her gold-streaked brown hair was smoothed into some kind of fancy roll at the back of her head. She wore a gray suit, the skirt just touching her knees. And underneath the suit, a cream-colored camisole.

She breezed into the kitchen. "Sorry that took me so long. I don't usually dress up, but I have to be in court today. And I couldn't find my pink camisole."

He poured coffee in an identical cup to hers. No mismatched mugs in Bayley's pristine white house. As he handed her a roll, her fingers brushed his. His stomach clenched at the simple contact.

He sat at the table and took a bite, Bayley watching him intently as he chewed and swallowed. "It's good."

"Thank heaven." She sagged into a chair. "I made chocolate-chip cookies last week that the Ice Pilots could've used as hockey pucks." She grinned and dug into her own roll. With her mouth full, she said, "You said you needed a statement?"

"Yeah. Tell me what happened yesterday in your own words."

"I was sweeping the deck when I saw what looked like a person swimming. The way his head kept going under I thought he was in trouble. I really thought I saw a hand wave, but now I know it was my imagination."

"So, you took off for the water and swam out to him?"

"No. First I screamed like mad for someone to call 911."

Cruse grinned. "I know that part."

"I knew he was dead when I saw him up close." Her face softened, sobered, and she set down her roll. "But...I kept thinking, he had someone who loved him, someone who would always wonder what happened to him if I didn't bring him in." She shrugged and met his eyes, the blue of hers vivid against the soft gray of her suit.

"You called him Harold." His voice held a question.

Her cheeks stained pink. "I had to call him something. It didn't seem right to keep thinking of him as 'the dead guy.'"

Cruse's lips twitched as he tried to hold in a laugh. "So you named him."

She studied her cinnamon roll intently and mumbled something incoherent.

"What?"

Her eyes met his. "After my great-uncle Harold. He's dead, too."

He laughed out loud. So long and hard that she finally started to chuckle a little, too. He took a swallow of his coffee to quench the last of his laughter.

The laughter faded from her face. "What was his name?"

Under ordinary circumstances, Cruse wouldn't have told her. At least not until he was certain the next of kin had been notified. But Slayton was on his way to notify and after her heroic act yesterday, Bayley deserved to know the man's name. "Brad Paxton."

The color in Bayley's face drained in an instant. "Brad Paxton. Are you sure?"

"As sure as I can be. His fingerprints matched. Do you know him?"

Bayley hesitated. "No."

"Bayley, come on. You know something."

She walked her plate to the sink. He held his tongue and finally she turned around. "I guess it doesn't matter now. If he's dead he can't hurt her."

Cruse narrowed his eyes as Bayley paused.

"His wife is at Hope House. He abused her and their daughter. They've been there almost two weeks. My court appointment today is—was—to get a restraining order against him."

That explained Bayley's court appearance. And gave the deceased's wife a motive for murder. "I'll need to talk to her."

"You'll need to take me with you."

"Bayley, this is a murder investigation." Not to mention spending the day alone with Bayley could really test his new "resist temptation" motto.

"And I'm the only person in this town who knows where she is."

"I know how to use a phone book," Cruse countered. "I can find your shelter." Civilians involved in a murder case inevitably fouled things up and Bayley looked bent on interfering.

"You'll find the address for my office in the phone book. For our clients' safety, the address of the shelter isn't published. In fact, it's a closely held secret." The tilt of her chin told him she wasn't budging.

"But you'll take me there to talk to Mrs. Paxton."

"Under the circumstances, yes. Or I could bring her to my office if you'd rather."

"No, I want to talk to her as soon as possible. Let's go."

He followed her out the door with a very bad feeling in his gut. If he eventually had to arrest Mrs. Paxton, he was not going to enjoy going head to head with Bayley. Especially when a fired-up Bayley made it tough to think straight.

"A couple of weeks ago, Brad came home late, like two in the morning." Melody Paxton's voice quavered. "He was shaking, and he'd been drinking. I thought he'd been in an accident or something. I've never seen him like that. If I didn't know better, I would have said he was scared, but that lowlife was too mean to be scared."

The woman's brown eyes were huge and haunted as she replayed the night she left home. One hand shook as she fiddled with an earring, the other white-knuckled the edge of the scarred table. The kitchen of the Victorian-house-turned-shelter was cozy, but that did nothing to dispel the notion that old ghosts were visiting today.

"Something happened that night?" Cruse's voice was gentle.

Melody hesitated and Bayley moved instinctively closer. She knew the drill, but sitting here listening, even knowing the interview wasn't directed at her, a knot settled in her stomach. She couldn't count the times she'd been in exactly Melody's position—answering questions she didn't understand about events that were beyond her control.

With every inquiry the police leveled at her that implied she'd somehow been responsible for her stalker's sick fixation, her confidence had wavered. But it was that same lack of understanding for victims that led her to raise funds for Hope House. To become the director of the shelter and an advocate for those who could not speak on their own behalf. God had given her a mission with these women and their children, and work she could be proud of.

One day Melody Paxton would know that feeling. The

feeling of living without fear, and having a life she could celebrate.

"Melody?" Cruse prodded gently.

Melody stared at her fingers, tangled in a knot in front of her on the table. "I asked if he was okay, and he went off. He hit me over and over again. Even in the face. And he'd always been careful not to leave marks on my face." She half laughed, the hiccupping sound closer to a sob. "Cara—my four-year-old daughter—heard me crying. I could hear her begging him to stop, but I couldn't see. I thought he'd broken my cheekbone."

She stopped and swallowed hard, her eyes turning to her little girl outside in the yard, the bitter look on her face softening. "He broke her arm that night. It was the first time he'd ever touched her." She shook her head. "I could take it. But when he hit my baby…"

The mother swiped the lone tear that escaped down her bruised face. "I thought I'd cried as much as I could."

Bayley put her arm around Melody and squeezed. "You're doing great, hon."

"I knew I had to get out. As soon as he drank himself into a stupor, I took Cara and we left. We had nothing but the clothes we were wearing. But we have each other. And now I know God's taking care of us." She sent a shy smile Bayley's way, before she went on.

"I went to Bayley's office the next morning, and after we took Cara to the E.R., I haven't left this building since two weeks ago yesterday. So I didn't kill him, Detective." She straightened in her chair, anger and dignity on her battered face. "But I promise, I wish I'd been the one that did."

Bayley cleared her throat. "We have video surveillance of the grounds, Cruse. We can prove Melody didn't leave."

Cruse made a note on his small pad. "I'd like to see those. Melody, what do you know about Save Our Shores?"

The blonde snorted and limped to the wide window that overlooked the backyard. "I blame them for this. When he got them as clients, he was so excited because he knew he'd have a lot of billable hours. We'd take vacations, he said. After a few months, he started coming home spouting off about how we're destroying natural habitats. That the politicians didn't protect our coastline, that money was the only thing they would listen to. But that S.O.S. had ways to make them listen. He was always a little on the edge, but they turned him into a real nutcase."

"Did you ever meet any of his associates or friends?"

Melody's shoulders lifted with a weary sigh. "He kept all that separate, but a few weeks ago on a Monday, a guy came to the house looking for him. He was sweating and kept looking behind him like he expected the boogeyman to jump out of my bushes. His name was Freddy Hughes."

"If you think of anything else, will you give me a call?"

Melody turned to Cruse, her face relaxing, finally. "Yes, of course."

Cruse stood and tucked his notepad into the back pocket of his jeans. "You've been a big help. Thanks for taking the time to talk to me."

Bayley left Melody in the kitchen where she could keep an eye on her daughter and walked Cruse through the living room to the front door. "Thanks, Cruse, for being gentle with her. She's been through a lot."

Cruse shot her a surprised look. "Did you really think I would grill her?"

She stopped and took a good look at him. His tanned, honest face, his true eyes. Her heart squeezed just a little. Maybe she did think that, and she hadn't been fair. He'd done nothing to deserve her mistrust. "No, I just— Thanks."

"No problem." He hesitated like he might say something, but stepped back, cop face firmly in place. "See you around."

Bayley let her gaze rest on Cruse's broad shoulders as he got in his Jeep and drove away, an uncomfortable prickly feeling settling on her skin. She could handle a cop. Lord knew she had enough practice at that. Handling the man…a man who slid under her defenses and made her feel, that was a different matter.

When Bayley settled in her own car and checked her insistently beeping cell phone, she had four messages from her assistant wondering when she'd be coming in to the office today.

She drove the few short blocks from the downtown house that served as a shelter to the building—strip mall, really—that housed her office, where she met clients and spearheaded her fund-raising efforts. The clients were her heart, but she couldn't keep the shelter open if she didn't raise the funds—a skill she *had* learned from her mother, who had never baked a day in her pampered life.

As Bayley breezed into her office, her assistant Stacy jumped up from behind her desk in the receptionist area, sleek dark hair swinging. "About time you got here. And you've been keeping something from me," she singsonged.

Oh, great. The story of her rescuing a dead body must have already spread. Nothing like living in a city that despite its size had the gossip mill of a small town. "I was going to tell you, I just haven't had time yet."

"Oh, please. Well, I want details now. How long have you been seeing him? What's his name? There wasn't any card, I checked." Stacy gave her an impudent wink.

Obviously, she and Stacy weren't on the same page at all. "I have no idea what you're talking about, Stace."

She walked to her office door and stopped cold. The roses dominated her desk. An involuntary shudder shook her as she quickly counted. Eleven. *Oh, dear God, please, no.*

She forced herself to breathe with her chest constricting

and whirled back to Stacy. "I'm going to Starbucks for a cup of coffee. When I get back, I want those things in the Dumpster out back. I don't want to talk about them. I just want them gone."

"But—"

Panic welled and Bayley forced it back, forced herself to stand there and look Stacy in the eyes. "Gone. Please, Stacy, just do as I ask."

She couldn't stay any longer. The roses in the office loomed behind her, taking on a life of their own. She hurried out the door, inhaling deeply as warm sunshine reached her face.

He's in jail. He can't hurt you. She repeated it like a prayer as her feet carried her hurtling away from her office.

She knew he couldn't hurt her. So why did she have this horrible feeling in her gut that her stalker's reach had suddenly grown so much longer?

THREE

Cruse slid the drawer back into the file cabinet with a hollow clang. "Empty," he said unnecessarily. "Every last one of them has been cleaned out."

Slay leaned back in Brad Paxton's wooden desk chair, making it creak and groan. "Here, too." He held up a paper clip. "Unless you call this evidence. Someone beat us here, and didn't want to take any chances that we would find something in the files."

The office was oppressive—the shades had been pulled, presumably for privacy, but the wood-paneled walls created a dark box and stirred Cruse's unease. He had passionate feelings about close spaces. He hated them.

Brushing a fingertip through the dust that the crime scene unit had left behind, he said, "So we've got nothing. We've had nothing before. Let's get out of here."

He pushed away from the file cabinet and headed for the door, but not before he caught the amused look from his partner. Slay knew about Cruse's loathing of narrow spaces, but he also knew better than to mention it if he wanted to keep his face intact.

Cruse jumped into his Jeep, shifting into gear as Slay settled beside him, sliding on Ray-Bans against the late afternoon sun. "CSU said the house wasn't the crime scene. The investigators lifted fingerprints which may give us a few leads, but I have a feeling we're not going to lack suspects in this case—Paxton had some first-class enemies. And that's just counting the ones I've read about in the newspaper."

"No kidding." Slayton grimaced. "We're gonna have to wade through the background of every person who ever attended a Save Our Shores meeting. Not to mention every person they ever threatened. I'm getting a migraine already."

Slayton's cell phone rang. "Slayton Cross." He listened for a moment. "Go ahead."

Hot wind blew through the Jeep, whipping Cruse's hair, a relief after the confines of the Paxton house. Even in the middle of summer, he preferred the top down. Open air and palm trees—even traffic noise—were preferable to dark memories of being closed in.

His own cell phone rang and his hand went automatically to his belt to silence it. "Conyers."

"Cruse, this is Edgar Foster, Bayley Foster's father. I heard about the murder victim my daughter pulled out of the ocean yesterday. I'm concerned about her safety."

Glancing behind him, Cruse eased into the other lane, only to have it slow. "I don't think you have anything to worry about."

"My daughter was stalked over a period of years and brutally attacked only months ago, Conyers. Forgive me if I don't share your attitude."

Cruse had known about the stalking and attack in the nearby town of Pensacola, and as a local cop, had been kept abreast of the situation when the family spent time at their beach house, which was rare. When the high-profile case closed, it had been all over the news. If he remembered right, that guy had gotten fifteen to life.

The older man sighed. "I'm worried about my daughter, Detective. I've asked around about you and I understand you have a very good reputation." The grudging tone in his voice didn't quite negate the compliment.

Gritting his teeth, Cruse reminded himself the man was his sometime neighbor and Bayley's father. "Mr. Foster, is there a reason for your call?"

"I'd like to pay you to keep an eye on my daughter when you're not on duty."

"I'll be glad to watch out for Bayley, but I don't want any payment." He shifted into gear, pressed the gas, got an answering growl from his Jeep's engine as he surged into the passing lane.

"Nonsense. Of course you should be compensated for your time."

For Cruse, keeping his beach safe was a personal quest. And he sure wasn't going to take money from Bayley's father to do something he would do out of his conscience anyway, no matter how uncomfortable. He tried to speak very clearly. "I'm happy to keep an eye out for Bayley. But I'm not going to take money from you." He couldn't resist a slight jab. "After all, isn't that what neighbors are for?"

"I'd prefer to keep this a business arrangement."

"I wouldn't."

Bayley's father went on as if Cruse hadn't even spoken. "I'll assume that you will keep watch on the house and check on Bayley periodically?"

Looking out for Bayley would put him squarely in her life. A place he didn't want to be, a place dangerous to his "no attachments" philosophy. He sighed. It was so much easier to fall back on old habits, and being a loner was definitely a skill he'd cultivated.

"Conyers? Can I depend on you?"

"Mr. Foster, I said I'd watch out for her, and I will."

"Thanks. I'll drop a check in the mail to you tomorrow." Foster hung up. Cruse resisted the urge to bang his head on the steering wheel. A car behind him honked.

"Trouble?"

Cruse had forgotten Slayton was in the car. "No, just an annoyance. How about you?"

"News. We got ID on the first victim from dental records. His name is Frederick Hughes."

"No kidding." Looked like his instincts had been on target. A carload of bathing suit–clad girls waved, elbowing and giggling, as traffic started moving again. He didn't remember ever being that young.

"What do you know, Cruse?" Patience wasn't exactly Slayton's strong point.

Cruse pulled into a parking space outside the police department. He turned to look at Slay. "Our murders are linked. And the common factor?"

"Let me guess. S.O.S."

Bayley spied an opening and slid into the beach traffic. She'd been mad at herself all day for letting Scott Fallon get the best of her with those silly flowers. She'd called her attorney, who would report him to the prison authorities, for all the good that would do.

She needed to be home, needed the sound of the surf to soothe her frazzled nerves. If she hurried, she could make it. This time of day, traffic was slow, a stream of people headed down Highway 98, but she pulled into her driveway just in time. Grabbing her favorite beach blanket from the clothesline tied between two wooden stilts under the house, she settled on the edge of the small dune at the foot of the home— and watched glorious color spear across the evening sky.

A soft breeze whispered through the sea oats, almost a reminder that God was in control, a reminder of His presence. She wasn't alone, had never been alone. She breathed in the fresh air—the lingering scent of coconut-scented sunscreen, and the lighter salty scent of the water—and let herself feel strong and healthy. She'd made it. And that was what she needed to remind herself today. A stalker could mentally torture her—or try—but he couldn't touch her.

The sun dipped below the horizon and darkness seemed suddenly to drop around her. She hurried to her feet, folding her blanket. She fought the urge to look behind her, nervous after the roses today and the possible Peeping Tom from last night. But how pointless was that, when her stalker was miles away? Maybe if she told herself enough times, it would sink in.

She stopped to pick her shoes up from the base of the stairs where she had left them and climbed barefoot to the door of her home. Digging for her key, she dropped one shoe from where she had shoved them under her arm and chuckled. *Waiting for the other shoe to drop…*

She unlocked the door to her house and pushed it open, turning back to pick up her shoe. When she stood, she saw it on the table—a single rose, the blood-red color of her fear.

A strangled cry escaped her throat as she dropped what she held—the blanket, her purse, her other shoe. She glanced frantically around the house, but the dark, silent and heavy, kept her from seeing into the corners of the room.

She wouldn't be reckless, but she'd lived in fear too long to let him win now. Taking a deeper breath, she flipped the light switch on. Warmth poured into the room from the overhead lights. Then she saw what she hadn't noticed.

The gift, wrapped in a shiny white box with a red satin ribbon, lying on the table next to the rose.

She knew better. She knew she should leave it and call Cruse to come pick it up, but she had to know. Her skin crawled with foreboding, but she reached for the box, slid the ribbon off and opened it.

Her mind blanked, her emotions shutting down, as she realized. He'd been in her house. Not just to leave the rose and the gift, but he'd been in her house, in her dresser drawers. He'd touched her clothes, her lingerie.

Her pink silk camisole was wrapped tidily in tissue paper, a note tucked inside. Her breath coming in short gasps now, she picked it up, opened it.

Scrawled across the paper, the words *You're mine.*

Deep breath—no, she *wasn't* his. She closed her eyes, said a prayer that didn't bring immediate peace, but reminded her to be strong.

Squatting down, she clawed through her purse and finally found her cell phone. She scrambled back on hands and knees into the corner of the kitchen, keeping an eye on the door, wishing she had her gun right then. Her hands shook as she tried to make sense of the numbers scrolling across the screen. After what seemed an eternity she found the number and pushed Send.

"Conyers."

She closed her eyes at the sound of his rumbly voice. That voice shouldn't have the ability to make her feel stronger, like she wasn't alone, but it did. For some reason, it did.

"Cruse?" Her voice shook and she hated it, hated the fact that her heart rattled in her chest, and she'd broken out in a cold sweat. Most of all she hated that a person had the power to make her feel afraid. To make her rely on someone other than herself just when she was beginning to feel strong, to *be* strong.

"Bayley? What's wrong?"

Bayley took a deep breath and tried to quell the fear that coursed through her. "He's back. Cruse, my stalker's back."

Bayley managed to collect herself in the four minutes it took Cruse to arrive. She heard the wheels of his Jeep skid to a stop in front of her house.

"Bayley!"

She brushed away the trails of frustrated tears with the back of one hand as he barreled up the stairs.

"Bayley!"

"I'm here, Cruse. In the swing. I didn't want to mess up the crime scene inside any more than I already had." She gripped the hard, cold steel of her gun in her lap in what were now steadier fingers.

He slowed to a stop at the head of the stairs, looking at her with a combined expression of concern and compassion. She looked away. Could she even describe how it made her feel to call him for help? To feel like she had no other option?

Cruse came to sit beside her, the porch swing rocking with his weight. "Are you okay?"

"Yes."

"What happened?"

"Can I start at the beginning?"

"Please."

Bayley clenched her fingers around the butt of her Glock. She would stay calm. Letting creepazoid Scott Fallon have control over her was out of the question. "You know about my past—the whole stalking thing, right?"

Of course he did. He was a cop and this was his town. He'd probably even been briefed by her security team when she'd visited the beach. At his nod, she continued. "This morning, after you left, I went to my office. When I got there, someone had sent me roses. Eleven of them. I knew it was him because he still likes to torture me."

"I thought the guy was caught after the attack. Shouldn't he still be in jail?"

Bayley opened her eyes, a bleak feeling of inevitability nearly overwhelming her. "Jail can't keep a stalker from contacting a victim. There are a thousand ways he could have ordered those flowers."

"What did you do with them?"

"I had my assistant throw them away." At Cruse's frustrated growl, she quickly tried to justify her actions, even though she knew better. "I'm sorry. If I'd known what was going to happen tonight, I wouldn't have. But I was so unnerved, I just wanted them out of my sight."

"Why don't you tell me the rest of the story?" Cruse's strong shoulders took up more than his half of the porch swing, plenty broad enough to share the burden of her stalker.

"Tonight when I got home, I found the twelfth rose on my kitchen table, along with a gift box. In the box, my pink camisole, the one I thought I'd lost." She drew a shuddering breath. "He's been in my house, Cruse."

He strode into the house through the open back door, his tightly leashed grace reminding her of a predatory cat. Bayley trailed behind him and stopped just inside the kitchen. "There was a note." She gestured to it on the table.

Cruse's mouth set in a grim line, his feet planted. "Have you touched these?"

"Yes." As his expression darkened further, she pushed back her shoulders, apologized again. "I'm sorry. I know better."

She couldn't quite stay in the room with the evidence of intrusion on the table. The swing had been her place of refuge since childhood—the swing in her backyard, and the swing here at the beach house—and she retreated to it now, leaning her head back against the seat. It had been the place she ran when her fears overwhelmed her. She hadn't had a peaceful childhood.

The difference between then and now was as a child she had felt totally alone. Today she could pray and knew she wasn't on her own. And up to now, she had felt in control for the first time in years. She wouldn't let Scott Fallon take that from her. She couldn't.

Cruse crouched in front of her and placed a warm, heavy hand on her knee. "I called Slayton, Bayley. He's on his way here. He'll take the flower and the box and find out anything he can about where they came from, and see if there are any fingerprints on the note."

Crime scene investigators, fingerprints, threats, cops. Fear. All so familiar and so unwelcome now. She clung to the tenuous control that she'd had since Cruse arrived, but couldn't help burying her face in her hands. "I'm strong. I can handle a lot."

She didn't know if she was telling him, or trying to remind herself. "But I don't know if I can go through this again."

The swing rocked perilously as he sat down again and gathered her into his very strong, very big arms.

Bayley should be wary, shouldn't she, of the warmth and safety that beckoned to her in his arms? She didn't want to depend on anyone but God for strength. She especially didn't want to depend on this man who drew her so inexorably. He was a danger, a cop, another protector like her father and the seemingly hundreds of men who had guarded her over the years.

She didn't want a keeper. She wanted autonomy.

So why did she still cling to Cruse's steady, sculpted arms?

Because tonight she needed to borrow some strength when she couldn't help but think that the terror hadn't ended.

It was just beginning. Again.

Cruse paced the floor of Bayley's pristine kitchen, the cordless phone to his ear. At the end of the lap, he peered around the corner into the living area, where she had finally fallen into a fitful sleep on the couch. He didn't want to be here, should have been anywhere but here, with her, getting involved in her life. He'd always been able to keep his job and his personal life separate. Until Bayley. What was it about her that made it impossible for him to stay away?

"No, Slay. I don't want to wait until tomorrow to contact the prison. I want to know tonight if that guy is still there, who's been visiting him and who he's been calling." He sighed, picking up one of the hundred framed pictures of Bayley as a child that sat around her parents' beach house.

"Look, just do your best, okay? Bayley's holding up, but this is bound to be hard on her and the more information we can have, the better."

After getting Slay's agreement, Cruse had one more request from Bayley. She'd just gotten her freedom. If her parents knew this, she'd be back under guard in two seconds. "Keep this under the radar. The last thing we need is another high-profile case. We're going to get enough grief from the S.O.S. thing."

Cruse hung up. He still held that picture of Bayley. She'd been tan and adorable as an elementary kid. Adored her whole childhood if the number of photos were any indication. He hadn't known her then, not even from afar. What would it have been like, to have been a kid with parents who cared? He'd certainly never had that, been that kid.

Replacing the photo, he walked the length of the kitchen again to check on Bayley. He leaned against the door frame and studied her. She looked so young in her jeans and pale-blue T-shirt, no makeup, her hair still damp from her shower. Her full bottom lip trembled just a bit as she breathed. When he'd answered her phone call, he had raced to her house, not knowing what he would find. He'd already gone above and beyond, telling himself he was just being a good neighbor. It was his beach, his responsibility.

He could pretend that he was doing this as a favor to her father, or out of some sense of duty. But truth was, in the past two days, she'd surprised him more than once. He liked her spirit and he liked her spunk. He hated seeing that bruised look in her eyes and the wary trust as she'd asked him to help her keep the secret. Probably the reason she'd called him instead of 911.

How freaky was that? She depended on him to protect her. No fooling himself, he did a fine job shielding every other person that lived in a twenty-five-mile radius from harm. It was those who were the closest to him that he couldn't seem to protect.

An hour later, he sat on the love seat that matched the white canvas couch where she slept, staring at the window that, rather than showing the view outside, reflected what the room held. He heard Bayley stir, then glanced at his watch. 9:30 p.m.

She sat up, blinking her eyes against the light, hair mussed, and he fought the urge to offer comfort again. He didn't figure she'd appreciate it now.

Pushing back into the corner of the sofa, she curled her legs underneath her. Her face was hidden by a curtain of golden brown hair and when she spoke again, he could barely hear her voice. "I'm so tired of being scared."

"I know." What could he say? Bayley needed reassurance, and he was the only one here to provide it. "And I know that you were just getting back to a normal sort of life. It's only natural that you would be shocked by this happening now. You have as much courage as anyone I've ever met." He hesitated, wanting to say more, not knowing if he should.

Bayley wrapped her arms around her legs and rested her chin on her knees. "Thanks, Cruse. I know in my head I'll be fine, but the rest of me wants to run like mad."

"I know." And he did, but what he knew wouldn't make her feel any better. So, he couldn't help her get over her fear, but he could distract her. "How would you like to head into town and get some coffee? I happen to know a great place."

"I'd love to get out of here for a while."

So would he. In fact, he needed to get out of here, because what he was seeing reflected in that window was a man attracted to a woman that could and should never be his.

* * *

Driving along the coast on the way home, Bayley reached a hand out to touch Cruse's shoulder. "Thanks for taking me to your sister's coffee shop. I needed it more than I knew."

"Not a problem." His words were short, but after a slight hesitation, he covered her hand with his.

Business, Cruse. Keep it business. Bayley was creeping under his guard. Creeping. Yeah, right. She'd slipped right under that famous guard when she'd crawled out of the ocean last night.

He cleared his throat and flipped the blinker on, easing his Jeep into a turn. "So. About tonight. I'll stay with you until we can get—"

She was already shaking her head. "No. There's no way I'm having anybody in my house."

"Bayley."

"Don't use that tone of voice with me. I'm not giving up my privacy because of one incident. I've got the best security system, the best locks, and to top it off Thomas is next door. You're next door to him. I'll be fine."

Cruse clenched his fingers around the steering wheel. He should have known she'd be difficult about this. "That's not close enough and you know it."

"No."

Cruse reined in his temper and took a deep breath. "Bayley, let's be logical here. If this Fallon guy is directing events, he already tried to come after you once."

"I know that." She stabbed at the air-conditioning controls, turning the fan on high. "The alarm wasn't on today because I left in a hurry. He's not going to take the chance."

"Are you willing to gamble your life on that?"

"Yes. I can't give up control over my life in a snap because of those flowers. Please try to understand."

Cruse pulled into Bayley's driveway, opened his door and got out, leaning on the open door. "I do understand. But—"

"Please don't ask me to give up my freedom, Cruse." Her softly voiced request got to him far more easily than her obstinacy had. Cruse glanced sideways and saw that she'd looked away, her eyes making contact with the ground.

He backed away from pushing her further. "Come on. I'll walk you up and check out the house."

Cruse climbed the stairs to Bayley's deck, inspecting both neighbors' houses as he did. Mrs. Phillips's house was dark, but Thomas Stanfield reclined in one of his deck chairs next door on the other side. The man waved as he saw them. Bayley gave him a distracted wave back before unlocking her door and turning off the security system. No warning flashed on the security panel but Cruse checked through the house anyway.

He crossed the room back to Bayley. "It's clear. Are you sure you don't want me to stay?"

Bayley took a deep breath. "I'm sure. I'm worn out and all I want to do is go to bed and sleep."

Against his way better judgment, he headed for the door. "I'll see you tomorrow. Don't forget to reset the alarm."

She nodded wearily. He closed the door behind him and stood on the deck, looking out over the beach. The surf rolled in soft curls tonight, the nearly full moon making the sand glow.

Thomas Stanfield still sat outside. Cruse didn't know the younger man well, even though the beach community tended to be very tight. The Stanfields kept to themselves.

No way around it—Cruse didn't trust the guy. No matter what Bayley thought about Thomas Stanfield, it seemed too convenient to him that Stanfield had gotten into town yesterday and the stalker reappeared today. Cruse crossed the deck to stand facing him. "I'm Cruse Conyers."

Stanfield looked Cruse over for a minute before replying. "I remember. Good to see you again. Hey, is Bayley okay? She looked a little distracted."

Cruse searched the younger man's eyes. Nothing showed but shadows in the dim light. "She's had a rough couple of days."

The man shook his head. "She doesn't need this right now. She's been through so much. I'll keep an eye on her."

Yeah, that's what Cruse was afraid of. Impatience simmered. The calls he'd made to try to track the stalker's movements had only made him more antsy for action. Tomorrow would have to be soon enough, though, because he already had plans for the night.

He said his goodbyes and walked down the outside stairs of Bayley's house to where his Jeep sat in her driveway. Once in, he pushed the seat all the way back. Bayley may not want him in the house, but she didn't say anything about the driveway.

He'd walked away from his sister believing she would be fine. And he'd been so wrong. He'd let her down, left her to defend herself against a stronger, meaner enemy. He couldn't walk away from Bayley, not with memories of his sister, Sailor, so present even today.

Somehow he would keep Bayley safe, not because her father had asked, but because he wasn't letting another woman get hurt on his watch.

FOUR

Bayley lay in bed watching the fan turn lazy circles on the ceiling, the glow of the full moon through her plantation shutters better than any night-light. She'd had decaf coffee. There was no reason for her to be wide-awake at three in the morning. Her legs jumped, her heart raced. Her favorite Egyptian cotton sheets stuck to her skin.

She kicked the sheet to the end of the bed and sat up. She wasn't afraid. Was she? Granted, the events of the day had been unsettling, frightening even. But she was locked in her house. No worries. So why did her nerves seem to be doing a supersensitive dance across her skin?

Maybe a relaxing cup of chamomile would work. She hadn't bought any, but her mother, the tea fiend, probably had some in the pantry.

Moonlight lit her way to the kitchen, but a premonition took her past the windows to check outside. She peeked out onto her deck. And jumped back when she saw a dark figure in one of her sunbathing chairs.

Bayley snatched the cordless phone from the kitchen wall, her finger on the nine before her mind registered what she'd seen. Moonlight glinting off sun-bleached hair. Cruse.

She'd told him she didn't want him inside her house, so he slept on her deck instead. In a bent-up, neck-cricking position in a too-short plastic chair. Foolishly, tears pricked her eyes. She'd had a lot of protectors over the years. Most of them paid by her father, starting when she was a little girl.

Edgar Foster, a lawyer, represented some very, well, controversial clients. He'd had death threats for years that he regularly ignored, but when a kidnapping attempt was made on four-year-old Bayley, he set up guards outside their East Hill home in Pensacola.

None of those guards had cared a lick how she felt about them being in her space. But Cruse did. And he wasn't even being paid to care. Like everything, though, even the best intentions sometimes came with repercussions.

Bayley pulled another cup out of the cabinet and began brewing the chamomile tea. Her parents were people who attended church because it looked good on their social résumé. They didn't understand her desire to go to the little church she attended in the not-so-suitable part of town. Her desire to be independent, even in that decision, and her staunch insistence that God had His hand on her life.

And now, here was Cruse, doing what he wanted, despite what she'd asked him to do. Her instincts said trust him, but everything she knew, everything she'd experienced in her life told her to run from this man.

Cruse jumped to his feet as she came out the back door, but settled quickly back into a sheepish lump. "I was hoping you wouldn't catch me. I tried sleeping in the car…"

She handed him a cup of tea and sat down on the chair beside him. "You didn't have to stay."

He glanced up from his mug to meet her eyes. "I know. But, after your day, I wanted to make sure you had a peaceful night."

"Seems like you're constantly coming to my rescue."

"Nah. It would make me look bad if anything happened to you in my neighborhood. I'd never hear the end of it from the guys at the department." He took a big sip of his tea. "Ugh. What is this stuff?"

"Chamomile."

"It tastes like grass."

"Probably because it is. It's supposed to relax you."

"This view ought to work a lot better than that grass in your cup." He placed his mug on the tiny round table between their chairs and walked to the deck rail. At three in the morning, the moon had traveled across the sky and angled across the water in a rolling ribbon of light.

Bayley joined him at the rail. When she glanced up at him, he wasn't looking at the moon anymore. His eyes were on her face. A long piece of her hair, floating in the breeze, brushed Cruse's cheek. He took it between his fingers and very deliberately tucked it behind her ear, his fingers sliding along the sensitive skin on the curve of her neck. He leaned toward her.

In the bright moonlight, she could see his eyes dilate as he gazed into hers. He didn't move away, just stood, a breath between them.

A splash of a fish jumping broke the silent spell. Cruse stepped back and flicked a glance out toward the ocean.

The mood broken, Bayley looked down at her cup of tea. "I—"

"Maybe you'll be able to sleep now," Cruse interrupted her and stepped farther away.

Oh, sure she would. "Maybe so."

She took a few steps toward the house. "Cruse, there's really no reason for you to stay. Please go home."

"I'm fine here. It's a beautiful night."

"Well. Good night then."

"'Night."

Bayley walked through the kitchen door and closed it, pressing her back against it. The sense of danger had shifted away from the constant anxiety she knew so well. This new fear startled her in its intensity—that the walls that she'd worked so hard to build around herself could be breached so easily by a cop who gave up his good night's sleep for her to feel safe.

"So did you find out anything interesting?"

"What?" Cruse looked up from the sheaf of papers he was studying to find Slay sitting on the edge of his desk with a donut in one hand and a steaming cup of coffee in the other.

"That *is* one of the S.O.S. files, isn't it?"

"No." He hesitated and shifted in his seat. "It's a background check on Bayley's neighbor, Thomas Lane Stanfield."

"Really?"

Cruse shoved Slay off the desk and onto his feet. "Yes, really." Cruse frowned. "I don't know why I requested it other than a hunch. Something's…off about him."

Slayton shrugged and reclaimed his seat on the edge of Cruse's desk. He took a bite of donut and talked around it. "You've got good instincts no matter what that report says. So who is he?"

"Only surviving son of Charles Hutton Stanfield. In the family business, Stanfield Development. The company buys large parcels of land, develops a neighborhood concept, and sells the lots to builders at a markup. Works for them. They have properties all over the south. Big ones in Atlanta, Birmingham, here along the coast."

"Interesting. You think he had something to do with the roses yesterday?" Slayton's eyes skated around the room.

"Who knows? But there's nothing here to throw up any red flags." Cruse tossed the file on his desk, discontent and little sleep making him restless.

"Maybe not, but we should definitely keep our eye on Stanfield the younger." Slayton turned a sly look on him. "Kind of like you kept your eye on Bayley last night?"

"Shut up, Slayton." Stepping away from Bayley last night had been one of the hardest things he'd ever done.

"I talked to the warden at Century Correctional Facility. Scott Fallon has not only had no visitors lately, he hasn't made a single phone call in weeks."

"He still could be responsible." Cruse stood up and pointed at the twelve-inch stack of S.O.S. files. "Can you focus on those today? I'm going to prison."

A little over an hour later, Cruse walked through the doors of Century Correctional Facility, where convicted stalker Scott Fallon was spending his incarceration. Slay's information didn't mean Fallon didn't pay one of the other inmates to send flowers for him, but it certainly raised enough of a question in Cruse's mind that ultimately it sent him to interview a man he'd rather never lay eyes on.

Cruse sat in a room that could have been any visiting area in any prison, no less depressing for its familiarity. He could never understand what would make someone choose a life of crime when this place was the consequence of it. No easy buck could possibly be worth spending years here, confined.

The door clanged open and Bayley's stalker shuffled in. In his orange jumpsuit, he looked almost waiflike, a shag of thin brown hair falling across a gaunt face, characterized by prison pallor. He looked young—barely old enough to vote, much less spend the next fifteen years locked away.

When the man was handcuffed to the table across from him, Cruse spoke. "I'm Detective Cruse Conyers."

The sullen look remained in Scott Fallon's eyes.

Cruse kicked back in his chair, all easygoing nonchalance, the opposite of the tightly strung felon sitting opposite him. "I'm here to talk to you about Bayley Foster."

Sullen turned to bitter on the convicted man's face and he spat out, "What makes you think I want to talk about her?"

"Why wouldn't you? I mean, by all accounts, you've been obsessed with her for years."

Fallon closed his eyes and when he opened them again, Cruse saw dejection, anger, even defeat. "I'm not obsessed with her. We had a relationship."

Cruse snorted. "Yeah, the kind of relationship where you end up in prison for assault with a deadly."

Fallon threw his hands up in disgust only to have the cuffs catch and clank on the table. "Fine. Think whatever you want. I don't want her now anyway. She had me put in jail."

Only years of practice keeping his face neutral and his emotions in check kept Cruse in his seat as Fallon spewed venom about Bayley. He wanted to reach across the table and choke the life out of the predator sitting across from him. Men like this terrorized women and then got what amounted to a slap on the wrist before they were out and free to prey again. The man who assaulted his sister was only the first of those Cruse had the misfortune of meeting. He hadn't been the last. Scott Fallon wouldn't be the last, either.

The guard looked through the window. Fallon immediately slumped back in his chair, rested his hands on the table. The same hands that had stabbed Bayley, sending her to the hospital to fight for her life. Cruse couldn't change what happened to Bayley in the past but he sure could affect her future, starting by throwing Scott Fallon off balance.

"Bayley got flowers yesterday."

Fallon's gaze snapped to Cruse's. "What?"

"Roses. What do you know about them, Fallon?"

Scott Fallon sat up straight, surprise and innocence all over his face. "Nothing. I swear."

Could he possibly be that good an actor or was he telling the truth? "You could have sent the flowers from here."

"I didn't. I had my phone privileges revoked day before yesterday. I don't care, either. Not too many 'friends' or family members want to hear from the neighborhood pervert. That's what they think of me, you know."

"You could have had someone else call."

That stopped Fallon for a second. "Yeah, you're right. I could've. But I didn't." He looked around the room as if there were someone there to overhear. His eyes, an odd yellow-brown, lasered in on Cruse's. "I admit, I've played some mind games with her. She sent me to prison. But, dude, I'm killing time until I'm up for parole." He leaned forward, and spoke more quietly. "Do you know what they do to guys like me in a place like this?"

Cruse forced himself to sit still and hold Fallon's eyes. "I've got a pretty good idea, yeah."

Fallon glared at Cruse. "Then you know I'm not lying when I say I wouldn't do anything to jeopardize my chances at parole. You ask the warden. I'm, like, the model prisoner these days."

He jerked his hands up, showing Cruse the handcuffs. "I'm not getting anywhere near Bayley Foster. Got me?"

Do you know what they do to guys like me in a place like this? The words reverberated in Cruse's mind as he studied Fallon's face, the sheer desperation lending them credibility. "Yeah, I got you."

I'm not getting anywhere near Bayley Foster. Could Cruse afford to trust the words of a convicted felon?

Could he afford *not* to take them at face value? Because if Fallon's words were true, that meant there was a stalker still out there. And he knew exactly where to find Bayley.

Bayley dipped her roller in the lemon-yellow paint and rolled it on the wall, making a satisfying swath of color. Slowly but surely she would rid the house of the bland white furniture and accessories her mother had chosen for the beach house. Even the dishes were solid white, for heaven's sake.

The yellow paint would make an eye-popping contrast to the bright red and blue pillows she'd bought for the white sofas. The beach house had been beautiful; now it was going to be beautifully lively. Her taste, not her mother's. Bayley's mother was sweet, but always, *always* infuriatingly proper.

They'd never lived in this house much anyway. It had been bought as an investment and used to placate clients. She'd never had much chance to enjoy it except for that one weekend in college before the stalking started.

She'd tried desperately to fit in with other college-age kids, but she'd spent all her time with babysitters and bodyguards. She didn't have much in common with teenagers. They'd spent the weekend drinking beer and partying, while she'd longed to have a bonfire and roast marshmallows. It had been the last time she'd tried that approach to making friends.

She had a better method now. A church family, a community of people who allowed her to be just one of them, a person with faith, a person trying hard to find the right path, and not a victim, or her parents' only child. She had friends at work, and even a few women who had come through her shelter.

Bayley climbed the ladder to reach the top of the wall to blend the rolled area in to the area she'd already outlined. As a kid, she'd been a society girl with no friends except Thomas, her next-door neighbor and as much a loner as she. She wiped her forehead on the sleeve of her T-shirt. Warm, humid air poured in windows open for ventilation.

Rolling paint to Jimmy Buffett blaring from her iPod speakers, she created a smooth block of color. She stretched up to reach the very top and the roller tumbled out of her paint-slippery hands and hit the plastic tarp beneath her with a slap. She giggled and stepped off the ladder, reaching down for the roller.

A knock sounded at the door and she jerked her head up.

It stayed light late during daylight saving time and Cruse, dressed in full police department fineness, stood on her deck. She let the roller drop with a plop and brushed her fingers over her cheeks and hair. Her ratty shorts and old sorority T-shirt weren't that attractive, but she was painting. And he hadn't called first. He hadn't called at all today. Not that she was waiting for him to. Or had even thought about him unrelentingly all day long. She hadn't.

He knocked again. "Bayley, come on. I know you're in there. I brought coffee."

Clearly, the man knew how to bribe his way into her life. Into her house, she mentally corrected. She muted the music and opened the door.

He held out a to-go cup of coffee. "Decaf, sugar-free, fat-free vanilla latte."

She shouldn't let the fact that he remembered what she ordered the night before influence her, but she couldn't help a little thrill of gratification that he did. He might eventually be on that short list of people she considered a friend. Not that he seemed to think of her that way and maybe it was safer—her being a part of his job.

Taking the first swallow, she closed her eyes in appreciation. She opened her eyes to find Cruse watching her, amusement in those glass-green eyes of his. "What?"

"Oh, nothing. It's just that I think I've found the way into your affection. Who knew it would be a cup of coffee?"

"Let's get this straight right now. The coffee has found its way into my affection."

Cruse pulled on her lopsided ponytail. "Point taken. So what are you doing?"

"Painting."

"I can see that. Why?"

"I'm tired of boring. After I finish the yellow in here, I'm going with orange in the kitchen. And fuchsia for my bedroom."

Cruse flicked a glance at the bedroom door and Bayley felt a little tingle start at the base of her spine. She cleared her throat. "As long as you're here, you might as well paint."

She walked to the kitchen table where her supplies were laid out. Brushes of all shapes and sizes, painting pads, rollers of every thickness. She'd bought it all, having had no idea what she would need.

Cruse picked up a brush. "I guess the guys at the hardware store love you."

"I wasn't sure what would work the best. I've never done this before."

"You've never painted?" He took a closer look at the wall she just completed. "You're doing a good job."

She knew she was, and the thrill of being able to stand back and enjoy something she'd created with her own two hands was huge. But somehow hearing it from Cruse made it real.

He dipped his brush in the yellow paint and started edging around a window. "I came by to talk to you. I need to tell you something that might be hard to hear."

Bayley's stomach flipped. She put down her coffee, picked up a brush and dipped it in the paint. "What?"

When Cruse hesitated, Bayley said, "Cruse, just spit it out. I'm not fragile. I can handle whatever it is."

"I went to see Scott Fallon."

Bayley stopped midstroke. "Now, why would you do that?"

"Slay did some research last night after you found the flowers and gift. Fallon didn't make the call, and he hasn't had a visitor in weeks. So I went to see him just to feel him out."

She took a deep breath, held it steady. "You didn't tell me you were going."

"I didn't know it until this morning. Besides, what good would it have done? You already assumed he sent the flowers." Infuriatingly calm, he kept painting, not even looking at her. "If I confirmed it with my visit, you wouldn't ever have to know I went to see him."

"Okay, here's where we differ in opinion. It's my business where you went because it deals with my life. I've been sheltered from decisions since childhood and I'm through with it. You got that?"

Cruse blinked. Obviously he never imagined she would be upset that he interfered without her knowing. And that would be because he was a know-it-all, overbearing, stomp-all-over-her-wishes, hyperprotective cop. She *knew* he would be this way.

Cruse put the brush down and ran a hand through his surfer-blond hair, the same hair that kept throwing her off balance, making her forget what he was. "Bayley, I wasn't deliberately keeping you out of the loop. I'm here right now, aren't I? I just went to the prison this morning."

Bayley resisted the urge to punch him. "Fine, Cruse. What did you find out?"

"This is the hard part. I'm not sure he did it."

She went still. And took all the feelings tumbling through her—the fear, the anger and confusion—and packed them away. "Tell me."

He stretched a hand out as if he might touch her. And part of her craved it. The other part thought she might shatter if he did. His hand dropped. He shrugged. "I can't give you anything concrete. But in my career, I've talked to a lot of criminals. Yeah, some of them are psychopaths and you can't tell when those creeps are lying, but this guy… Bayley, I believed him when he said he didn't do this."

"In one interview because of some hooey sense of knowing things, you think you have him nailed? The Pensacola police hunted for him for years. He's smarter than he looks."

Cruse went back to painting, the brush leaving bold yellow strokes on the wall. "It's an easy leap to make that Fallon's the one starting the stalking business again. And I know what this sounds like. I shouldn't even be talking about it with you because there's no evidence—absolutely none—to back me up. But—" he stopped midstroke and turned to face her "—it's your life that's in danger, and I can't take the chance with it if he's telling the truth."

A tiny bit of her anger chipped away. He was concerned for her. He did tell her about Fallon, even though he didn't have to. She pressed her fingers to her eyes, looking down at her hands when they came away with a yellow streak. "Okay, what next?"

"I've got to work tonight. But I'd like to get together soon and go through this from the beginning. Are you up to that?"

She wasn't sure, but she wasn't admitting it. "Of course, just not tomorrow night. I'm going to church since it's Wednesday."

"I could go with you."

Bayley was already shaking her head. "You don't have to do that."

"I'll be going to church anyway."

A man of faith? So they really did exist. More of her wall of resistance crumbled, but with effort, she shored it up again. "I'll meet you here after church—around eight."

He laid the brush down and took a step in her direction. She thought he'd lean in to her, but he didn't. He gently removed a smudge from her cheek with his thumb. She swam into the ocean-green of his eyes. Last night he'd been this close to her and instead of walking away he'd come closer, tantalizing her with the idea of what kissing him would be like. He was thinking of it, too. She could see the memory of that moment in his eyes.

"Bayley, we'll figure this out. I don't want you to worry about it. This will end."

He crossed to the door and hurtled through it before she

could get a word out. The amazing thing about it, when he said it that way, with conviction in his voice and his heart in his eyes, she believed him. She just didn't want to believe *in* him.

FIVE

Clanking and banging sounded from inside Bayley's house.

Cruse unsnapped his weapon and stepped to the side of the door, knocking with the back of his fist. "Bayley, it's Cruse Conyers. Open up."

A couple of more pinging knocks, then silence. Cruse stood back, fingers twitching. What was going on in there?

The door slammed open and Bayley, with another lopsided ponytail, grinned at him, rust and some disgusting black stuff all over her T-shirt. She backed away as quickly as she'd opened the door, beckoning. "Come on in. I'm kind of busy, but we can talk while I finish up."

Cruse followed Bayley into the kitchen. The walls glimmered the brilliant color of orange juice. But what caught his attention were the components of her sink—faucet and handles, other assorted pieces—scattered in a semicircle around Bayley's rear end.

He cleared his suddenly dry throat. Deep breath, look away or *help*. Definitely offer to help. "Can I help you with that?"

She peeked her head back out. "Do you know how?"

"No. Do you?"

An impish grin appeared on her face. "Nope. But I looked it up on the Internet."

She disappeared under the sink again. He squinted into the

narrow space. Two people would be nose to nose, way too close. Two people would definitely *not* fit under there. He leaned against the cabinet next to the sink, hummed a bit of "Amazing Grace" under his breath.

He stole another look at her. "Uh, Bayley, are you sure that's a good idea?"

"What, fixing the sink?" With a wiggle and a twist, she tightened a connection and backed out.

"Doing it yourself with instructions from some guy named Joe-Bob off the Internet."

"Have a little faith in Joe-Bob." She turned on the water, which seemed to work perfectly. Cruse peered under the sink. No drips. Apparently Joe-Bob knew what he was talking about.

"Oh!" She jumped to her feet and rummaged through a bunch of plastic bags from the home superstore. "Aren't these knobs for the cabinet doors cute? They match the new knobs on the sink. And look…I bought a cordless drill!"

She flipped around to face him, planting her feet and brandishing the tool like a weapon. She revved the drill and flashed a grin at him that had his heart landing somewhere near the tops of his shoes. This woman took on life with both hands and feet.

Shaken, Cruse struggled to find equilibrium, reminding himself he didn't get involved. He protected, he solved cases, he moved on. Period. Wasn't that what he felt God asked of him—that he serve others?

He tried to smile back at her, but knew it was a lame try.

Concern quickly replaced the teasing look on Bayley's face. "Cruse, are you okay?"

"Sure. I'm just tired. It was a long day." He cast a fleeting look out the window at the crystal-clear aquamarine water. He'd give just about anything to be out there on the waves right now.

"I can't imagine. Not only do you have a murder investigation, now you're stuck with a neighbor who can't seem to keep herself out of trouble. How about a cup of coffee and we'll sit down to talk?"

She put the drill away while he began filling mugs from the coffeepot. He was a coward to let her think it was work that had him out of sorts. No way would he tell her the truth, though, especially since he didn't know what the truth was.

His heart turned with turmoil. He didn't want to get involved with Bayley, but everywhere he turned, it seemed that God was putting her in his path. There had to be a reason for it. Even in his new faith, he could understand that.

"You're turning into a good friend, Cruse," Bayley said as he slid the pot back into place.

Cruse's mind snagged on *friend*. Could it be that simple— that he felt friendship for Bayley? In the past, straightforward, uncomplicated affection wouldn't have even been a consideration for him. There hadn't been room for friendships growing up. His house hadn't been a safe place to invite schoolmates.

But still, friendship he could handle. Maybe.

More settled, he grinned at her, bringing a smile back to her face. He passed Bayley a mug and she curled up on the floor in front of the coffee table. Multicolored puzzle pieces covered the gleaming surface of the wood, the puzzle about one-third complete.

Cruse settled opposite her. He didn't want to bring up the stalker, which he knew would be hard for her, but he needed information. "Bayley, I'm sorry that we have to get into all this."

She scrunched her nose at him. "I know we have to discuss it at some point, so where do we start?"

"Let's see if any old memories might relate to your current situation. When did the notes and flowers begin the first time?"

"Just after Christmas break my junior year."

"How were you spending your time?" Cruse took a swallow of his coffee.

Bayley picked up green outside-edge pieces of the sunflower puzzle and tried them one against the other. "About the same as usual, I guess. All the required social events, pictures in the paper at whatever benefit my mother hosted, a couple of holiday balls. We flew to Aspen for the actual week of Christmas."

When Cruse raised his eyebrows, she continued.

"Wealth comes with its own set of rules and expectations, Cruse. My dad's a lawyer. He couldn't, or wouldn't, take time off from his practice if we stayed in town. So my mother instituted the Christmas trip when I was about seven. What about yours?"

"We didn't have Norman Rockwell Christmases." Cruse frowned into his coffee. His Christmas memories included his mother sleeping off a drunken stupor, but that image was far preferable to the one a couple of years later when she brought some strange man home after last call at the bar. He didn't talk about his mother. Ever. "Not the skiing-in-Aspen kind of Christmas, either. It was pretty much like any other day for us."

"I'm sorry."

He was, too, but the sorry didn't come from the lack of tree or gifts. He missed having a family, a history, people guiding him, teaching him to make the right choices, so he wouldn't have so many regrets.

He'd run from God for more years than he could count because he thought he couldn't change. And now he knew the truth. God hadn't been asking him to change, not on his own anyway.

He picked out a couple of the straight-sided pieces of the puzzle and tried them against hers, sliding a grin her way when the green leaves of the sunflower began to take shape. "So tell me about these parties. Who did you go with?"

"More than likely Thomas Stanfield. We had kind of a standing agreement about those things. At least if we had to suffer through some stuffy party, we'd have the other one to— Oh, wait. I didn't go with Thomas that year, although he was around. I can't believe I'd forgotten that. I had a boyfriend, Frank Williams. Thomas didn't approve because he thought Frank was a jerk.

"I didn't believe him. I was all caught up in the emotional whirl of having a boyfriend for the first time. At any rate, Frank didn't stick around long after the stalking started and the bodyguards reappeared. Too weird for him." She hitched a shoulder. "He obviously wasn't that important. I'd almost forgotten him."

Cruse straightened. "Wait a minute. You said the bodyguards *reappeared*. You had guards before?"

"And my dysfunctional childhood is relevant, why?"

"This started a long time ago, Bayley. The stalker reappearing now isn't some isolated event. Understanding your childhood might help me get a grasp on why this is happening now."

She'd gone stiff and defensive, but he leaned closer to her, silently encouraging her.

She pressed her lips together in a stubborn line. "I told you my father's a lawyer. He has always represented some controversial—and very powerful—people in political circles. Consequently, he got threatened. A lot."

"So you had bodyguards your whole childhood?"

"From the time I was four. My father never worried about his own safety, but some men tried to kidnap me when I was four, to make my dad back down from a case he was trying." She didn't look at him, her attention firmly focused on two bright yellow pieces of the puzzle.

She said it so nonchalantly. *Some men tried to kidnap me,* but in that instant, a child's innocence had been stolen forever, making the woman she was today even more amazing.

"Did it work?" That morsel of information could be significant. An unsavory client, or disgruntled losing opponent, who would stoop to kidnapping a four-year-old child wouldn't hesitate to sic a stalker on a young woman to get her father's attention. Definitely something to look into.

"Nope. My father hired 24/7 protection and kept right on trying cases."

Cruse didn't have a father and he probably wouldn't ever be one. But if he had a kid, that kid would know she was the most important thing in the world. And he wasn't sure he wanted to sympathize with her old man and his check-writing ways.

"You have to understand. My father thought he was making the world a better place. In the end, that would benefit me and everyone else's children, too." She shrugged. "I'm not saying he was right, it's just the way it was. I've made peace with him."

"So anything else you haven't told me…any other kidnapping attempts, attempts on your life during your childhood?"

"I didn't have a childhood, Cruse. There were no pajama parties, no pep rallies, no bonfires, no dates. Nobody wanted a kid around that came with her own bodyguards. Can you imagine?"

She flung a black puzzle piece down on the pile. "That's why I was so desperate to go to college. I stayed in a secure dorm, but I could have a life, make friends. But by then it was too late. I was too different. I'd never had all the shared experiences that other people had. And then when the stalking started, back came the bodyguards, and back I went to Daddy's protection. It was all over."

"It stunk, basically."

She stared at him a moment and then, to his relief, let out a half laugh. "Yeah, basically."

That so explained who she was—the vitality, the grabbing on to life with both hands, the desire she had to experience…*everything*.

No dates, she'd said. No dates meant no good-night kisses. Could she possibly be that innocent? He should stay away from her starting now. Yesterday. Last week.

Cruse focused on the puzzle, butting one piece up against another until he found two that fit perfectly. Even that made him think about Bayley and how they might fit together. How had they found each other, two people who didn't fit, who'd never fit? He would have judged her harshly if she hadn't just shared her story. He would've been wrong.

She was like him, trying to find where she fit, putting together puzzles that didn't seem to have all of the edges, tossing questions to God and hoping for answers.

He got to his feet, restless energy sending him wandering around the room. It was different. Something—the family shrine. All the photos of Bayley but a few of her with other people were gone. "What did you do with the photos?"

"I put them away in a box for my mother. They're hers. Her attempt at making us look like a typical family, I guess."

Bayley's college yearbook caught his eye on the bookshelf. He picked one and told her to flip through it while they talked. Maybe a picture would jog a memory.

"So where did you go to college?" Bayley asked.

"I worked my way through University of West Florida at night. When I got my degree I went to the police academy."

"Why'd you decide to be a cop?"

"I never thought of being anything else."

Bayley flipped a page in the book from her sophomore year. Then she tried again. "Yes, but *why?*"

Because he knew that what happened to his sister

happened to other people, too, and if he couldn't get *that* loser, he could at least put away someone else's. "Let's just say…I had reason to know that there are a lot of bad guys in the world. I wanted to take as many of them off the streets as I could."

She waited, an expectant, impatient look on her face, but he kept his mouth clamped shut and she got the hint.

Bayley yawned like she did everything else—voraciously. Shoving the yearbook aside, she stood and stretched her arms overhead. "If I'm going to keep at this, I need at least one more cup of coffee. You?"

"Yeah, sure." Cruse picked up the yearbook, trying to look anywhere but at the attractive and appealing woman across the room. A fuzzy gray photo of someone who looked familiar grabbed his attention, but he couldn't place him.

When it clicked, he smothered a gasp of surprise, glancing sharply at Bayley to see if she'd noticed. His mind told him it couldn't be possible, but sure enough, when he looked below the fuzzy picture, there—in indisputable black and white—was the *last* name he wanted to see in the context of Bayley's unhappy past.

Slayton Cross.

Next morning, in the cozy kitchen at the women's shelter, Bayley held a fat-cheeked toddler boy on her hip as the mother, Angel, fed her tiny infant girl. Bayley'd brought her here to help her settle in at the shelter, to get away from an abusive boyfriend.

"Hi, Bayley." Melody Paxton spoke hesitantly from the doorway to the living room. "Do you have a minute?"

Bayley put the little boy down on the floor of the kitchen, handed him a pot from under the counter and a wooden spoon from the container on the stove for him to drum with. She winked at Angel. "If you can stand it, I can."

Angel's eyes filled and she spoke so softly she almost whispered. "Thank you."

Taking Melody's arm, Bayley drew her into the living room to sit on one of the sofas that had been donated by a furniture store. A hideous spring-green color, but comfort counted here, not to mention the price was right. Still, maybe a slip cover or even a new couch was in order with the generous money an anonymous donor had just given. "So are you holding up okay?"

"Fine." Melody's bruises had faded and she'd put on a little makeup, but she didn't look at ease. She looked...nervous, scared. Her eyes darted around the room.

"If you're worried that I'm going to make you leave, there's no hurry. You can stay as long as you need to."

"It's not that. The police have cleared the house." She stared at the fireplace, cold and black now, summer's heat long since arriving in the Florida Panhandle. "I don't think they have any leads. The people that Brad worked with, they're very careful people. Very powerful people. He never said, but he was scared of them. And someone is killing them off. That someone has to be someone even more powerful."

The toddler banging the pot in the kitchen added sharp punctuation to Melody's words. "The police told you they don't have any leads?"

"They said they're following every available avenue to find my husband's killer. I think that means they don't know anything."

Sudden insight pushed Bayley to ask, "Melody, are you afraid that these people might come after you?"

Melody turned her eyes to meet Bayley's. In them, Bayley saw, not just fear, but abject terror. And weariness. The exhaustion that came with fighting back created a bone-deep fatigue that Bayley could so identify with.

The woman reached down the bodice of her sundress and

drew out a small rectangular object. "I took this from the house. I only looked at what's on it for a few minutes to see if it was enough to keep Brad off my back. Kind of an insurance policy if he fought me on getting a divorce."

"What is it?"

"Files." *Bang* went the pot in the kitchen.

"And you want me to have this?" *Bang, bang.*

"I want you to give it to your cop friend. I want him to find the person that killed Brad. Because I'm afraid if that person thinks I know something, he might come after me next."

Cruse cut the crime-scene tape across the door to Frederick Hughes's house and stepped inside. The house, having been sealed for a few days, already smelled musty, and dust motes swirled in the light from the windows. When Slay stepped in behind him, Cruse said, "The crime scene unit came up with what amounts to nothing. So we search every crevice and cranny of this house. Knock on walls, search the floor, the attic, for any kind of hidey-hole. I don't care how stupid we look. There's got to be something somewhere that can give us a lead."

They had run down the hundreds of names that had been in the public files for S.O.S. Either nobody knew anything, or they were too afraid to say anything for fear they would end up floating in the Gulf of Mexico, too.

Slay nodded. "Let's start from the top down. I'll take the crawl space."

Cruse looked at Slay for the twentieth time that day, the question on the tip of his tongue. *Why didn't you tell me you knew Bayley?* But all he had was a photo in a yearbook and a feeling that something wasn't right. He needed more before he risked either his partnership with Slayton or, if even a hint of his suspicion got out, his partner's reputation. Especially since colleges are big. Not everyone knows everyone, or remembers everyone. One more reason not to put his partnership on the line with silly suspicion.

"All right, I'll start in the master bedroom closet." Closets were bad, but not nearly as bad as the breath-stealing closeness of the crawl space in the attic.

Cruse walked to the master bedroom, letting his eye slide over the things the owner had left behind, looking for anything that seemed out of place. A lot of police work involved pure sweat—finding witnesses, talking to people on the street. Hopefully out of the hundreds of pieces of information that they compiled, a thread would emerge. But what cops didn't like to talk about was that sometimes, when they had nothing else to go on, a cop's instinct about a suspect or a lead… Well, sometimes Cruse had to go with his gut to solve a case.

He stepped into the closet, making sure to leave the door wide-open. His eyes roamed the ceiling and the empty shelves. He pushed aside the clothes, what little there were, to check the wall behind. He pulled the pockets out of each item of clothing. Not even a ball of lint. Thuds and muffled complaining let him know that Slay was having the same luck in the attic.

An hour later, Cruse was rifling through kitchen cabinets. In the mix of plain off-white coffee cups sat a frilly teacup with hot-pink flowers painted on the side, reminding him of Bayley transforming her house from her mother's plain-Jane white to her own eye-popping color choices. Which made him feel like a total idiot because everything under the sun reminded him of her. A teacup. Cruse shook his head in disgust.

Slay gave an earsplitting whistle from the laundry room, sauntered in and threw a packet sealed in waterproof plastic onto the table. "Finally, something. Taped inside the front panel of the washing machine. Passport, driver's license, social security card, birth certificate and, most important, beaucoup moolah. All in the name 'Carl Anderson.' Our boy was ready to run."

"Now we have an alias. And if he had one, he could have had others. Have you got someone digging through his computer?"

Slay shot him a do-I-look-stupid-to-you look. "Of course. The techs had some trouble getting past his security, but it shouldn't be much longer."

Cruse threw the kitchen utensils back in the drawer and slid it home. "I'm done. Let's get out of here."

On his way out, Cruse made one last pass through the house, starting in the master bedroom. It didn't feel right. But he had checked, even the mattresses on the bed. His hand hovered over the light switch, but he turned and went back to the bed, searching underneath again.

He'd checked the slats already, checked it all. But there in the tiny crack between the carpet and baseboard, a slip of white gleamed in the beam of his flashlight. Cruse stretched his arm out full length and snagged a strip of paper.

When he looked at it, his mind said "phone number." His gut said "lead."

Back at his office, after spending approximately forty-two seconds on the Internet, Cruse whipped free a printout with the name Robert F. Wexler, an address in Destin and a map to the house. All information derived from one phone number on a slip of paper found in victim Frederick Hughes's house.

A quick Google search netted Cruse more info, like the fact that Mr. Wexler and Robert Wexler, Ph.D., were one and the same. And he happened to be an expert on the beach mouse, along with a couple of other endangered species. All of which could be related back to the Save Our Shores group.

Cruse pointed the Jeep toward Destin, his police scanner

background noise for the ride. Precious little had been garnered from any previous interviews, and Wexler's bios seemed to indicate a legitimate scientist. Maybe he could shed some light on the situation with S.O.S.

His ears sensitive to scanner speak—he could be totally involved in a conversation and still hear a call go out on the scanner—Cruse heard Bayley's address. His fingers whitened on the steering wheel as he punched numbers in the cell phone with the other hand.

She answered immediately.

"Bayley, are you okay?"

Bayley breathed a disgusted sort of half laugh in his ear. "Yeah, I'm fine. I came home for lunch and when I came out, my tires were slashed."

"I'll be there in, uh—" he glanced at the clock in his dash and the landmarks to judge "—less than ten."

Punching the end button on his phone, Cruse growled at the futility of the situation with Bayley. Logically, there were steps he could take to make her safer. Illogically, he knew she wouldn't go for any of them.

Concern drew Cruse's brows together in a scowl as he turned on Bayley's street, the oyster shells of the beach drive crunching under his wheels. Concern turned to question as he got closer to the driveway and noticed Slayton's SUV already parked there.

Cruse pulled in beside it, left his light flashing and got out, scanning the property for Bayley. He found her in the shadowy area under the house, leaning against one of the wooden stilts, talking with Slay.

He searched her face. She looked ticked off. She'd do. He pointed a look at Slayton. "I'll walk you to your car."

Slay hesitated and then nodded. "I'll see you later, hon. Let me know if you need anything."

"Thanks, Slayton. And thanks for keeping me company."

"Anytime."

Cruse took Slay's shoulder as they walked down the drive. "How'd you get here so fast?"

"Ever since the flowers, I figured an extra pair of eyes couldn't hurt so I've been driving by when I've been in the area. Today, I saw Bayley beside her car and it looked like she needed help. She said she'd called it in, and you were on the way, so I waited with her."

Cruse stopped beside Slay's open door and waited as his partner turned to face him. "Thanks."

There must have been at least a hint of what Cruse was feeling on his face because Slay stopped in the motion of getting in the car. "Hey, listen, Cruse, I'm not after your girl. I just thought it wouldn't hurt to have one more pair of eyes."

Cruse noted Slay's earnest expression, hoping Slay was telling the truth, wishing he could clear him here and now. "I know. And she's not 'my girl.'" He glanced back to where Bayley waited in the shade under the house, then shrugged. "We're…friends."

Slay flicked his gaze from Cruse to Bayley and back again. "Okay, if you say so." He slid all the way into the seat. "I'll see you around."

Cruse slammed Slay's door, his eyes following the luxury SUV down the beach drive. Watching out for Bayley, he'd said. It could be true.

Cruse couldn't let his cop's imagination run away with him. Having to choose between a woman he admired and a friend he trusted was untenable. He prayed that Slay was telling the truth. But he cared about Bayley and her safety too much to let it go without at least investigating the possibility that Slay and Bayley's stalker were one and the same.

Bayley walked up to where Cruse still stood in the driveway. "I interrupted your work."

"Nah. Why didn't you call me?"

"I didn't want to bother you. I'm twenty-five years old. Plenty old enough to handle this myself."

"I thought we were friends." He drew a deep breath, and threw an arm around her shoulders, tabling his troubling thoughts. "Next time call. So how do you feel about mad scientists?"

SIX

Bayley was so sick and tired of filing police reports that by the time they were finished with this latest one, a visit to Dr. Frankenstein himself would have been a welcome relief. She'd called Stacy to tell her she wouldn't be back after lunch and took the drive with Cruse instead. An hour later, they pulled into Dr. Wexler's driveway in an old Destin neighborhood.

Bayley heard Cruse let out a sigh of appreciation and, amused, watched as he salivated over the surfboard on top of a beat-up Isuzu Trooper. Cruse walked over to it, sliding a hand down the smooth fiberglass surface. He looked up at Bayley, eyes shining. "This baby is one sweet board."

A door slammed. Bayley whirled around.

"The fact that you two obviously have good taste in surfboards is the only thing keeping me from throwing you off my property." A man with unruly dark-brown hair stepped from under the porch overhang. His Hawaiian shirt and loose khaki shorts didn't quite fit with the steel beneath his words. "Can I help you?"

"Cruse Conyers, Sea Breeze Police Department." Cruse held out his identification for the other man to take. "This is Bayley Foster. We're looking for Dr. Robert Wexler."

"You found him. But call me Bo." He returned Cruse's ID and motioned for them to follow him into the bungalow.

Bayley's skin breathed a sigh of relief, entering the cool dark house. Relief turned to awe as she stepped out into a true Florida room, an indoor paradise that housed what looked like every plant native to this area of Florida and then some.

"Have a seat." Wexler gestured again, this time at a wicker patio set.

Cruse leaned forward to murmur in Bayley's ear. "Feel like I'm in the middle of the jungle. All he needs is some monkeys."

Bayley shot him a look and said, "Behave."

Wexler settled into a chair, which creaked under his weight. "So what business brings you to my front door?"

Cruse pulled out a small notebook. "I'm investigating a series of murders. I came across your phone number at one of the victim's houses. Frederick Hughes?"

Unsurprised, at least by the expression on his face, Wexler nodded. "I read about that in the paper, but I didn't know the man. That group he belongs to—Save Our Shores—they use my research occasionally."

"How do *you* feel about development of waterfront property?" Cruse's eyes narrowed in on Wexler's face.

The man smiled broadly and met Cruse's eyes dead on. "Clear the air, huh? I'm a scientist, Detective. I study what happens to the animals when development comes in. Watch the trends, watch the populations increase or decline. I record changes in the animals' behavior when their habitat changes."

Wexler took a breath, and paused, apparently gathering his thoughts. "I grew up coming here to my grandparents' cottage. I love the beach. There've been a lot of changes over the years. And some of it I'm not crazy about—like the traffic—but I'm not going to resort to the tactics that S.O.S. uses."

"You said they use your research. How does that work?"

"Someone comes to me with a specific plot of land they'd

like checked out for endangered species. I do a study, write up what animal life I find, write recommendations for the least invasive development. What they do with the information is up to them."

He shrugged. "There're more and more companies that want to help preserve the native environment. They know it's good for their business to take care of the waterfront. So, when I make recommendations for conservation, a lot of them follow through. They build farther back from the beach-front, build boardwalks across the dunes, stuff like that. But sometimes it all comes down to money and unfortunately money talks louder than I do."

Cruse leaned forward, a fiercely intelligent glint in his eyes. "And the particular piece of land you surveyed recently?"

"I'd have to check my copy of the report to be sure, but I can tell you this much. S.O.S. was very excited by what I found. This project is different because the developers want to use both sides of the international waterway. They want to use the barrier island for beachfront condos, and across the Sound, build a golf course resort. I didn't find anything unusual on the beach side, but on the Sound side I found the flatwoods salamander. As that habitat dwindles, so do the numbers."

Wexler's eyes lit with excitement. "There's been at least one recent case where a court order has permanently stopped construction."

Cruse leaned forward, a war-ready gleam in his own eye. "Which makes a powerful motivation for murder when you're talking hundreds of millions of dollars."

"Absolutely." Wexler tapped the table with his pointer finger and nodded. "So it looks like you've got yourself a motive. And just in case you were wondering, S.O.S. wasn't the only request I got for that piece of property. I assume it was the development company that requested, but the client's identity was protected through attorney-client privilege."

Cruse in action impressed Bayley. She knew cops—had been around plenty enough to know—and Cruse was a good one. He reached across the table to shake Wexler's hand. "Thanks so much for your time, Bo. Your help has been invaluable."

Wexler walked them to the front door and opened it. Cruse stepped over the threshold into the late afternoon heat before turning back to the scientist. "One more word, Bo. Be careful. These guys, whoever they are, are serious. I'd hate for you to get caught in the cross fire between the developer and the environmentalists."

Wexler waved a hand. "I play on this field all the time. I know how to cover myself. But thanks."

Bayley shivered despite the saunalike atmosphere of the summer afternoon. "I hope nothing happens to him," she said as she followed Cruse to the car. "He's a nice guy."

Cruse opened the car door for Bayley and paused to glance back at the house. "Yeah, I think so, too, but without a clear threat to him, warning him is the best we can do. Until I can find out who is behind that development project and get a list of viable suspects, Bo is going to be in danger."

"Maybe I can help with that."

Cruse shifted into Reverse but when her words sank in, he slowed to a stop. "What do you mean?"

"I was at the shelter today and had an interesting chat with Melody Paxton." Bayley dug down into her purse. "She gave me this. Apparently, she made a copy of all of Brad Paxton's files. Kind of an insurance policy if he tried to contest a divorce."

Cruse took the jump drive that Bayley handed him, the brush of his hand warm and familiar now. "Why didn't she give this to me the other day?"

"She's afraid. Apparently some of Paxton's friends weren't very nice people. Or it could be that she thought his death was too good to be true and wanted to be sure before she gave up the only leverage she had."

Cruse fingered the tiny storage device. "It wouldn't be a bad idea for her to stay hidden at your safe house until we find her husband's killer. If he thinks she knows something, she really could be in danger."

"I know. The stakes are getting higher by the day."

Bayley rode in silence in the passenger side of Cruse's Jeep. He drove with single-minded precision, though that didn't surprise her.

He flipped those gorgeous green eyes her way. "So, Bayley, what are you going to do now?"

Great. The question she'd been trying to avoid all afternoon. She decided to try nonchalant innocence. "About what?"

His shoulders stiffened. Her overprotective guy alarm started going off.

"You know what."

"Yeah, I do. And I'm not going to do anything, Cruse. Anything I do that changes my regular life just gives power to the stalker. I've done that. I'm not doing it anymore."

Cruse hesitated. "Bayley, maybe…maybe you should trust God. Trust…me."

She could tell it was hard for Cruse to say that. Sharing his faith had to be difficult, but even so, she didn't want to hear it. "Tell you the truth, Cruse, I'm tired of trusting. I think sometimes we have to learn to depend on ourselves. You know everything I've been through. How can you sit there and tell me to trust Him now?"

"Because I've let God down plenty of times in my life. I've learned it works out better when I trust Him. I know He doesn't let me down."

"I want to believe that, but the reality is I do feel let down, and very, very alone." She stared out the window of the car at Choctawhatchee Bay as they crossed the bridge from Destin back to Okaloosa Island.

"You're not alone, Bayley. Have you stopped to consider that God put you in the house on the beach two doors down from me, *and* brought me home from my assignment at the exact time when you needed my help?"

"Of course I know God gives me what I need, Cruse." She just wasn't convinced that it was Cruse.

Cruse sighed. "You do know that the slashing of your tires is escalating from sending flowers."

The muscles in his jaw clenched, a sign that he was close to losing his temper, she realized. "Yes, Cruse, I get that."

Abruptly his tone changed, went soft. "Can you do one favor for me?"

"What kind of favor?"

He laughed, still in that quiet tone, making Bayley smile against her will. He was up to something.

"I'm not telling you." His teeth flashed white against his deep surfer's tan. "Yet."

It wasn't until two hours later, when he'd shown up at her office with a hugeified German shepherd–something mix that she'd had an inkling of what he had planned. A rescue pound "puppy" with a mighty bark, Scruffy would stay in her house with her so that she didn't have to have other people invading her space. She sniffed once, tears threatening to overflow again.

Cruse had even told her that he hadn't really planned to get her a dog; it had been "divine intervention." He'd been racking his brain trying to figure out how to keep her safe, and he heard about Scruffy on the radio. A ten-minute spot the station did every week, trying to find homes for dogs who were down to the wire at the local pound. He'd listened, not only to the radio—a no-brainer—but to his heart and he'd put her and Scruffy together. They needed each other, Cruse had said.

And when she looked into the dog's soulful brown eyes, so eager to please, she hadn't been able to resist.

Bayley detested being afraid. She'd promised herself that once they caught the stalker, she'd never be afraid again. She'd make herself strong, and she had. But once again, time had taught her a lesson. Fear was a part of life.

She hadn't thought about it much at work, but home alone now in this empty house—well, she'd handle it. Casting a rueful look at the dust rag in her hand, she sprayed the gleaming surface of the coffee table and swiped it again. Scruff cocked his head at her.

Bayley grinned. When the stalking started again, she hadn't been sure she would survive a second time. And then came Cruse.

Cruse—of the golden-boy hair, the mesmerizing green eyes, and the untouchable attitude. She'd been sure he was another arrogant, overconfident cop like the hundred others that had crossed her path in the past four years. He'd pretty much confirmed her opinion with his mile-wide protective streak.

She'd thought she had Cruse totally pegged and then…then he gave her the dog. Scruff rambled closer and bumped his big lunky head against her thigh, before settling at her feet.

She'd tried to slam that door to her heart shut again, acting like she was mad at Cruse, but doggone if she couldn't even give it a halfhearted shove. He'd given her the one thing that would allow her to keep some measure of independence and still be protected. And he'd done it by giving her the one thing she'd always wanted and never been allowed to have. A dog.

Glancing around the living area, she sighed. Nothing left to clean. Every surface gleamed. She gave a low whistle that had Scruffy jumping to his feet. "Let's go outside, boy."

As she crossed to the kitchen to put her cleaning supplies away, she heard a low growl. Scruffy stood at the entrance to the kitchen, feet planted. The fur bristled on the back of his neck and he growled, deep and low, again, warning Bayley that she wasn't safe.

With her heart pounding double time, she snatched her handbag off the kitchen counter. She found her 9 mm, checked it and pushed the safety off.

Glass crashed. She hit the floor behind the counter, sliding on her stomach. Her alarm blared and the dog went ballistic. His deep, rough bark and the clamor of the alarm reverberated in open rooms of her house.

More glass shattered. Bayley, fingers shaking from the adrenaline—and yes, fear—got her cell phone out of her purse and dialed 911. When the operator answered, she told the woman, "Someone's trying to break into my home. They've broken the window, at least one."

She couldn't hear the operator over the noise, so she laid the phone down, leaving the line open. Taking a deep breath, she slowed her heart rate, and crawled low around the counter in the kitchen to where she could see into the living area.

Glass sparkled all over the floor she had just cleaned. The sheer privacy curtains were sliced from the jagged pieces and fluttered forward in the breeze through the broken windows. And on the floor lay three gray lumps, tied to bricks.

Sweat popped, a fine mist across her forehead, as nausea rolled in an instant through Bayley's system. She closed her eyes and swallowed hard. Dead birds.

Scruff stood over them, still barking like mad, looking like he wanted to go through the window after whoever had thrown them in. Bayley leaned back against the counter and tried to breathe through her nose to stave off hyperventilation and calm her unsteady stomach. "Scruffy, come," she ordered.

In a split second, Scruffy stood beside her, guarding her.

She buried her face in the soft fur of his side and waited for the police to arrive.

Within minutes, Bayley heard pounding on the door. She scrambled to her feet, picked up her cell phone, and said, "Someone's at the door."

The emergency dispatcher replied, "Yes, ma'am, the police are on-scene. Would you like me to stay on the line while you answer the door?"

Another deep breath. "No, that's okay. I've got it now."

Bayley closed her cell phone and looked out the peephole to see an officer she'd never met standing there, and had to stifle the quick surge of disappointment that it wasn't Cruse. The cop wasn't extremely tall, but built, and his shaved head gleamed in the porch light, matching the mirrored sunglasses he'd shoved to the top of his forehead. He didn't have his weapon out, but his holster was open, his hand hovering in the vicinity. He was twitchy, and she didn't blame him.

Scruffy stayed glued to her side as she turned off the alarm and opened the door. The cop looked warily at her dog, before turning his gaze on her. "Are you all right, ma'am?"

Bayley nodded. "Yes." She grabbed the loop of Scruffy's collar and held him. "I'm Bayley Foster. May I see some identification, please?"

The officer gave her a look, but reached into his pocket and pulled out his wallet and badge.

After a look, Bayley motioned the officer into the house. She could hear other boots coming up the stairs now. Reinforcements. "Officer Sheehan, I need to tell you that I have a handgun. It's on the counter in the kitchen. It's registered and I'm licensed to carry concealed in Florida."

Another one of his serious cop looks. "Did you fire the gun, Ms. Foster?"

"No, I did not."

The next fifteen minutes passed in a blur of questions,

cameras flashing, and cops tramping through her personal space. Alone for the moment, she stepped into the hall to stay out of the way. The tiny amount of control she'd felt cleaning had vanished and turmoil had rushed back in like a huge tidal surge. Bayley buried her face in her hands.

Cruse's cell phone beeped. Grateful for the excuse to leave the paperwork that every cop he knew hated, he picked up his phone, thumbing the button to recall the number—dispatch.

"Conyers."

"Detective Conyers, this is dispatch. Officer Sheehan asked that you be informed of a break-in at two-two-four-six Shellfish Drive, home of Bayley Foster."

Cruse ignored the uncomfortable squeeze in his chest as he grabbed his keys.

Only after he was racing full speed down the beach road to her house did he realize the feeling in his chest had a name. Terror. It was easy to say *have faith* and so hard to do when tested. He tried to pray, but only one thought, one prayer, came out. "God, keep her safe. Please, God, keep her safe."

Cruse hung on to his composure—barely—when he saw Bayley stepping out of the hall into her great room. He didn't say anything, but clamped down hard on the anger that filled him that someone would do this to her.

Dead birds—a sick prank? No, not with her history. It was a statement. *I killed the birds, I can get to you, too.*

He scanned the room. Glass shattered all over the floor, cops in plain clothes scouring the area. Joe Sheehan stood at the door, his massive arms crossed, an impassive look on his face. And Bayley, in the middle of it all with that mutt of a dog, looking like a woman who had it all together, like a woman who didn't need him.

She wasn't his sister. Even if the circumstances reminded

him of Sailor, Bayley was twenty-five and entirely capable of taking care of herself. She lifted her eyes to meet his. He raised an eyebrow at her, not trusting his voice.

"I'm okay. I'm not hurt, just kind of stunned."

Cruse listened as the cops on-scene reported their findings and then closed and locked the front door behind them, for whatever good that might do. He turned and looked at Bayley, sitting on the sofa, weariness and determination on her face. A flicker of satisfaction passed through him as he noted the dog sat motionless beside her.

Cruse sat down in front of Bayley on the coffee table. "You can't stay here tonight."

She gave him a sullen, almost angry look. "I know that."

Cruse grimaced. "Sorry. I didn't mean to state the obvious. What I should have said is, why don't I stay here and wait while you pack an overnight bag?"

"That's not much better, but you get points for trying." She stood and walked into the bedroom, the dog following half a step behind her.

He had the storm shutter down and locked over the broken window and most of the glass swept off the floor when she appeared in the bedroom door. Her leather overnight bag hung from one hand, and the smart-aleck eye-roller was gone, replaced by a waif of a girl who just looked scared. Cruse leaned the broom against the wall and took a step toward her.

She dropped the suitcase where she stood, and sobbing, launched herself across the room into his arms.

Cruse wrapped both arms around her and held her close, wishing there was a single thing he could do to make her problems disappear. He ran a hand up her back, cradling her to him.

With Bayley in his arms, he tried to remember all the reasons he walked away from relationships in the past. He needed to distance himself now. It had always been so easy, but he'd never had anyone like Bayley in his life, anyone who made him want to stay. How did a guy walk away from a woman like Bayley?

She sniffled and he held her closer, savoring the closeness, just for this stolen moment. Getting involved with Bayley would be impossible. Bayley was ski trips to Aspen and he'd never woken up on Christmas morning believing in Santa.

It had taken nearly thirty years for him to believe in God, that God could heal those hurts in his past. But even God couldn't make the past go away.

Gently, Cruse steadied her on her own feet and, with his thumbs, wiped the tears from under her eyes.

She had tried so hard *not* to need him. Seemed like maybe he and Bayley both had some hurdles to get over before they could do any real trusting.

Bayley followed Cruse as he shoved his way into the house, banging and bouncing off both sides of the door. He'd insisted on handling Bayley's overnight case, a twenty-pound bag of dog food and Scruffy's food and water bowls. Apparently, her soaking the front of yet another of Cruse's shabby T-shirts had brought out the Neanderthal in him. He'd been silent and stoic all the way home, that telltale muscle in his jaw giving her a clue just how grim he felt.

He dumped the bag of dog food in the kitchen and stalked down the hall, disappearing with her case into what Bayley assumed was a bedroom. She stood in the doorway and stared. Cruse's home was beautiful. She'd never have guessed it from that half-finished paint job outside.

A small house, the soaring ceiling with light-oak beams made it feel anything but close. He'd furnished it with large masculine pieces, obviously secondhand. Not one of them matched. She smiled when she saw the beat-up, scratched-up, obviously well-loved surfboard that graced the space over the fireplace.

Scruffy nudged her side with his nose. "I'm sorry, boy. I was being so nosy I forgot all about you." Bayley unleashed the dog, who promptly went searching out the smells of Cruse's place. Down the hall, a door clicked and Bayley turned to see a tall green-eyed blonde coming into the room with a load of freshly washed towels. With her hair swept into a smooth chignon at the base of her neck and her all-black attire, she was a chic female version of Cruse. Bayley would have known Sailor anywhere.

She laid the laundry on the sofa and came straight to Bayley with her arms outstretched. "Oh, sweetie. You've had such a night." Sailor wrapped her arms around Bayley and squeezed tight.

Bayley's eyes filled again at the tender concern. She swiped at them with her sleeve. She *had* to stop freaking out every time someone was nice to her.

She sniffed. "I'm Bayley Foster. But you obviously know that."

Sailor patted her arm. "Follow me. I think it's teatime."

In the kitchen, Bayley leaned on the counter. Sailor opened the cabinet door and pulled out a box of tea. "Where's my brother? I thought I heard him come in."

"He took the bags to our rooms, I guess."

Cruse strode into the room. "I've got some things to check on. I'll be back. Sailor, set the alarm."

He slammed the door behind him. Sailor looked at Bayley and burst out laughing. "What's up with him?"

Bayley shrugged and fiddled with the paper tag on her tea bag as Sailor poured steaming hot water into her cup. "I blubbered all over him when he tried to be nice to me after the other cops left. I think it pushed him over the edge."

Sailor dipped honey out of the pot into her tea before

sliding the pot over to Bayley. "If I know how my brother thinks, and I ought to by now, he's mad at himself because he thinks he should've been able to keep you from being attacked."

Bayley stopped her spoon in midstir. "He wasn't even there."

"I know that, but that wouldn't matter to Cruse. You matter, therefore he's responsible."

Sailor picked up her cup and gathered the laundry from the sofa. "I didn't have time to find clean clothes when Cruse called me to come over. I'm going to take these and go to my room, so you can have a little while to relax in peace before you go to bed. I think Cruse put your bag in the guest room on the right."

She whisked toward the hall door, energy in motion.

"Sailor…"

Sailor turned back, a question on her face, so like Cruse's.

"Thanks for being here, for coming when Cruse called."

"He's always been there for me. I wouldn't let him down for the world." She disappeared into the back hall.

Bayley wandered to one of the wide windows, nearly tripping over the dog in the process. So a few girl tears pushed the hot cop over the edge. She lifted a weary hand to rub the ache that had started in her temple. The distance Cruse wedged between them should be fine with her. Distance would make it easier to let go later when…well, just later.

She was good at letting go. Over the years, she'd become an expert at it. The bodyguards had become her pseudo-friends, but they weren't really. Uncle Leo, the one she'd had for ten years, had become the father her own had never been. Still, when he retired, she'd never seen him again. And then there was Carlo, the cute one, the big-brother type who brought her chocolates on her birthday. The day he left for the police academy was the last time she'd ever heard from him.

After Carlo she stopped learning their names.

So, yeah, she was used to letting go. She just happened to be tired of it. She'd even, lately, begun asking God to send friends who would stay in her life. And in her small church community, she had started to find them. It took time to build the kind of relationships that lasted, especially when dreams of friends had been another of those things she'd said goodbye to a long time ago.

A degree in counseling and a master's in social work had been part of her training for her job as the director of the shelter. She knew Cruse felt responsible—Sailor hadn't had to tell her that. Right now he was probably listing all the ways he could have protected her and didn't, even though he was at work at the time of the "attack." But that didn't ease her frustration at the strain between them.

The deck, and Cruse's screened porch, called to her. She walked out the back door and dropped into a soft man-style lounge chair, closing her eyes. The waves shushed on the sand, a constant murmur. As constant as God's care for her. Something she didn't take for granted, despite her frustration.

She rubbed the knob of scar tissue on her shoulder. *Reality check, Bayley. Yes, it's bad, but no one got hurt.* She could still, with the surf sighing in the background, find that small bit of peace that she knew was the gift of God's presence.

Maybe CSU would come up with something from her house, or Cruse would find some clue to the identity of this stalker. She really hoped so, because she couldn't take much more and whatever Cruse was up to, she didn't think he could either.

SEVEN

Weary to the bone, Cruse shouldered open the door of another bar, the doors of which had grown grimier and less appealing as the night progressed. Far from the posh side of town where Bayley grew up, this seedy area was his heritage. Some legacy. Despite his fatigue, he returned steel to his spine and straightened his shoulders along with his resolve. Surely someone somewhere in the stinking underworld of this city had to have information that could lead him to Bayley's stalker.

He'd left her at his house with two cops on guard outside, the best alarm system money could buy on the inside, partly because he needed answers. But he also wasn't sure he trusted himself anywhere near her as raw as he felt right now.

Letting his eyes adjust to the darkness inside the bar, he registered the stillness that accompanied his entry. Places like this, strangers weren't welcome. Then, he wasn't much of a stranger to places like this. Informants didn't exactly like coming down to the station. But his familiarity didn't come from meeting informants; it came from his childhood. He'd spent many nights hauling his mother out of bars. Maybe not this exact one, but the assault on his senses was the same. Blue-gray smoke hung in the air, along with the stench of men and cheap beer.

He recognized the bartender, a man many a cop had identified as being involved in some very serious illegal dealings, and one no cop had been able to pin anything on. Street name Cutter, the name indicating his singular skill with a knife and his willingness to use it.

Cruse eased onto a corner barstool, keeping most of the room in view and giving himself up-close access to Cutter. If the looks he'd been getting from the hard-core patrons of this fine establishment were any indication, he'd need to watch his back.

Cutter worked his way down the long bar to Cruse. He met Cruse's eyes with a blank stare. "Yeah?"

Cruse looked straight into the man's eyes without blinking, without glancing away. Neither did Cutter, though the skin at the corner of his left eye jumped. "I need information."

Cutter's shoulders relaxed and he let out a bark of a laugh, abruptly cut off as he locked gazes again with Cruse. "You won't be getting that here."

"I think I will." He leaned forward, palmed a twenty onto the bar. "See, here's the thing. I know you use this bar to set up your deals. Maybe I can't pin anything on you, but I can send the health and fire inspectors in here tomorrow and I bet they could find enough code violations to shut you down for a month, maybe two." Cruse looked the man up and down, from his greasy black ponytail to his steel-tipped black boots.

"I had you pegged for a cop from the second you stepped through the door," Cutter spat out.

"Yeah, I recognize a criminal when I see one, too. So do we talk, or do I call in the inspectors?" Cruse scanned the room as he waited for Cutter to answer. A guy shifted in the shadows at the far corner of the room, drawing Cruse's attention.

"What do you want?"

"If I wanted to hire someone to scare somebody, who would I talk to?"

Cutter let out a noise of disgust, crumpled the twenty in his hand and shoved it into the pocket of his black jeans. "Come on, man, any punk off the street'd do for that."

"No, this guy would be different. In and out, no trace. Probably good with electronics, alarm systems. Not afraid of getting caught because he thinks he's too good."

Cutter's eyes skittered to the right, to the other end of the bar, and back again. Nerves? Or something else.

"I don't know nothing, man. You're wasting your time here. And ain't none of these guys gonna tell you what you want to know."

Cruse looked into the dark-brown eyes of the bartender, a man who'd long ago sold out to the fast buck, easy ride. Bet it didn't seem so easy now.

Conversation stilled again in the room as Cruse slowly stood. Sarcasm leaked out of his voice as he said, "Thanks, Cutter, I'll be sure to remember how helpful you were tonight."

Cruse pulled the door open and stepped out into the dark, muggy night. No thunderstorm had relieved the unrelenting summer heat. Lightning crackled on the horizon, but from experience Cruse knew the welcome relief of the storm would not come tonight.

He reached in his pocket for his keys as he stepped near his Jeep. Two shadows loomed suddenly on either side of him, the snick of weapons being cocked bringing him to an abrupt stop.

"Cops aren't welcome here." The voice snarled, gravelly and harsh, as if it'd taken years of abuse from tobacco. "What did you want with Cutter?"

"I was passing the time. Came in for a drink just like you." Cruse waited for an opportunity. If he was patient, maybe it would come.

"Drink somewhere else." The man, whose face Cruse still couldn't really see, gave a barely perceptible nod.

Pain ricocheted through Cruse's head. He slumped against his Jeep. *Stay awake,* he commanded himself. He blinked twice trying to see around the swirling spots of his vision. He narrowed in on the one thing he could see—the man's big gold necklace with a two-inch peace sign dangling from it. How ironic.

Cruse focused his eyes just in time to see a meaty fist coming straight at him. He flung his head back and the blow glanced off his cheek. Black spots danced in front of his eyes again but he managed to reach into the back of his Jeep. His fist closed around a tow chain. Rage fueled his swing, and he knew a direct hit would do damage, maybe even kill his attacker.

But that *wasn't* who he was. It was who he might've been if he'd stayed on this side of town, if he hadn't allowed God to change his life. He might've been Cutter or any of those sad figures in that bar. But he *wasn't.*

He pulled his punch, felt it connect. His assailant staggered back, injured but not taken out. A blow from behind knocked Cruse to the ground. He vaguely registered his head hitting the pavement before the black, oppressive night reached down to swallow him.

Bayley let out a yelp as she took a gulp of too-hot coffee. That didn't stop her from going back for a second sip, though. She owed Sailor for starting the pot before she left for work.

She sank deeper into the oversize chair, relishing the view of the beach and the turquoise-green ocean beyond. No one knew where she was and she felt cozy and safe in Cruse's house.

Cruse, who'd apparently stayed out all night if the un-mussed bed in his room was any indication. Not that she'd had the nerve to go in there to check, but the door to what was obviously the master bedroom had been open.

Okay, so she'd peeked.

And just as she thought, there were sides to Cruse she'd never seen. His room, rather than being the earthy greens and browns that most men seemed to like, had been whitewashed and filled with splashes of color, from the bright-red spread on the bed to the vintage surfing posters on the walls.

The dead-bolt lock clacked open, followed by the insistent beep of the alarm, immediately silenced. Cruse.

Bayley burrowed deeper in the chair. She'd thrown her chenille robe over her shoulders and stumbled into the kitchen to make coffee. She winced, imagining her hair must look like a family of moles had made their nest in there. Yuck.

Luck must be blowing her way because Cruse walked right past her. Or more accurately, shuffled past her. As she watched him head toward the hall, he stopped, swayed and grabbed the counter for support.

She jumped out of her chair. "Cruse, what's wrong?"

"Nothing a shower won't cure." He turned to face her and she gasped, pressing her fingers to her lips. He tried to smile, but a cut on his lip opened and blood welled.

In three steps she was at his side, reaching out for him.

"Don't." The look in his eyes, more than the word, stopped her cold.

"Cruse, please let me help you."

He lifted his hand from the countertop, held it out as if to defend himself—from her—and swayed again. "Just let me…just let me clean up."

And he turned away.

He eased his way down the hall, skimming a hand on the wall for balance.

Bayley stood watching his painstaking way and tried to fight the feeling that he had slapped at her, had wanted to get rid *of her.* She kept coming back to that look in his eyes.

She wasn't the one who put that look there, or who had

caused him physical injury, the stubborn man. He took care of her, but he wouldn't let down his guard to let her even take a look at the cuts and bruises on his poor, beaten face.

She sighed. She couldn't decipher him. She'd claimed they were friends, but something inside her questioned it. Friends didn't treat each other like clients. Friends let each other help. What was he so afraid of that he wouldn't let her touch him?

An hour later, dressed and ready, she poured herself another—her last, she promised—cup of coffee. And jumped two feet when the phone at her elbow rang. She waited a couple of rings to see if Cruse would answer, but when he didn't, she picked it up. "Hello?"

"Hi, Bayley, can I talk to Cruse?" Sailor's voice sounded rushed, harried.

"He's kind of indisposed at the moment. Can I help you?"

"Can you find him? I'm in major trouble here at the coffee shop. My entire staff went out to eat together last night and got food poisoning! They're all, well, you know. I don't want to go into detail, but I need my brother—desperately! I know he's scheduled to be off this morning."

Bayley bit her lip. Cruse didn't look like he would be in any shape to work all day at a coffee shop. "Hang on, Sailor. Let me check and see."

Bayley stepped quietly to Cruse's door and knocked. As she did, the door opened slightly, but Cruse didn't answer. She bit her lip. Go in, or not? Gingerly, she peered around the door.

Cruse lay fully dressed, facedown across the bed, his blond hair still damp from the shower. Was he even breathing? She tiptoed close, and watched him. His torso rose and fell evenly—breathing, but not awake.

The way he liked to take care of people, he'd probably be furious if he let his sister down. But she didn't think she'd ever seen anyone ever in need of rest more than Cruse. He probably needed a doctor, too.

Executive-decision time. She wasn't going to wake Cruse, but that left Sailor in the lurch. She picked up the phone in the kitchen. "Listen, Cruse's asleep so…" she spied Cruse's keys lying on the counter where he had stopped to rest "…if you give me directions, I'll fill in, okay?"

Sailor's whoosh of relief reverberated through the phone line. "Honey, I think I love you. You have no idea what you just agreed to, but I'm too frantic to turn away help. I'll see you soon."

Sailor rattled off directions and the phone clicked in Bayley's ear.

She stood looking at it for a few seconds before taking mental stock. Today was an off day, no problem there. Shoes, hair, makeup. She was ready. But what about Cruse?

Looping her arm through the chenille blanket over the back of the sofa, she tiptoed back into Cruse's room. Awake, he always seemed so in charge, so powerful. In sleep, the silvery blond curve of his lashes brushed his cheek, making him seem vulnerable and somehow softer. Yeah, right.

She covered him with the blanket and lingered there for a second. A hesitant hand—could it possibly be hers?—stole out to brush over his bruised knuckles. Awake, he hadn't even wanted her sympathy. In sleep, his damaged hand reached for hers. *Oh, Cruse. Where have you been?*

She slid her hand from under his and strode to the door. With any luck, he'd sleep straight through and she'd be back before he ever woke up.

Still groggy from sleep, Cruse stumbled his way down the hall. His head wasn't spinning quite as much and he felt reasonably sure he could have a conversation with Bayley without hurling on her. He owed her an explanation, at least as much as he could tell her, and what little he could remember.

He reached for the coffeepot and found it cold. Something wasn't right. Bayley never turned the coffeepot off.

Cruse turned to scan the room, stifling a groan as his brain sloshed around in his skull. "Bayley?"

Cruse took off down the hall at a run—ignoring his head, his ribs, and every other part of him that threatened revolt.

The door to the guest room stood wide-open, the bathroom door, too. Cruse's heartbeat picked up. Wrong. Very wrong.

He rushed for the front door before he stopped himself. Blind panic wouldn't help Bayley. That knock on the head must have shaken him up more than he thought.

Come on, think like a cop. Turning a full three hundred and sixty degrees, he scanned the room. And forced himself to take a deep breath.

No sign of struggle jumped out at him—the furniture, the rugs—all were in place. Her coffee cup was rinsed and in the sink. She hadn't been forced to leave.

Unless she went with someone she knew. The thought speared through him like a hot knife. *Think, Cruse.*

The cordless phone caught his eye, sitting not in its cradle, but right beside the sink…as if she had hung up the phone, set it down, rinsed her cup and left.

He checked the caller ID. Sailor?

He hit Redial, paced the length of the counter while he waited for it to connect, and nearly slammed the phone into the countertop when he got a busy signal.

Keys. He needed his keys. Checking his pockets, he fought back the urge to swear. The extra keys were in the kitchen drawer. But when he locked the front door behind him, he found his driveway empty. The Jeep was gone, too.

Lucky for him he had another choice. He unlocked the

garage and slid open the door. His Harley sat waiting for him, just like he'd left it a couple of weeks ago.

Eighteen minutes later Cruse roared up to the back entrance of Sailor's coffee shop, Sip This, and closed his eyes in relief at the sight of his Jeep.

The panic shimmied back out to sea as quickly as it had come, replaced by one overwhelming desire: shake some sense into Bayley Foster.

He strode to the back door, which stood open as usual—terrible security—and stopped short when he caught sight of Bayley. She had one of Sailor's black Sip This aprons around her. The heat of the kitchen and steam from the coffee machines had made her hair frizz and put pink in her cheeks, and she absolutely glowed.

The dog, Scruffy, sat on a pillow behind the bar out of the way. He looked at Cruse, winking a sleepy eye at him, as if to say, "You're only just noticing?"

As they worked, his sister cracked a joke, and Bayley laughed, sliding a cup of coffee in front of one of the customers at the bar, and murmuring something to him that had him smiling and nodding, too. Why did she continually surprise him? He shouldn't have been surprised, but he was—to see the Pensacola society girl perfectly at ease waiting tables in his sister's beach coffee shop.

Cruse knew when she caught sight of him. A soft smile crossed her face, just a deepening of that dimple in her cheek, along with a look of mild concern. His aching ribs suddenly reminded him he hadn't even looked in a mirror before leaving the house. His face probably looked worse than his ribs felt.

Bayley dried her hands on her apron, spoke to Sailor and crossed to the door where Cruse stood—leaned actually—he didn't feel as steady on his feet as he would have liked. "I would've left a note if I thought you'd be up. You feeling okay?"

Cruse glowered at Bayley.

She narrowed her eyes. "What's wrong, Cruse?"

He spared a glance for the patrons of Sip This. "What's *wrong?* I thought you'd been kidnapped," he whispered hotly.

"Obviously, I wasn't," she said, her voice as frosty as his was heated. "I'm sorry I didn't wake you, but you needed rest and Sailor needed help. I thought I was doing you a favor."

She stalked past him into the center of Sailor's tiny courtyard. "I don't need protecting, Cruse. I'm a grown woman perfectly capable of making decisions. Anyway, don't you trust your sister?"

Cruse drew a breath as deep as his injured ribs would allow, willing himself not to shout at her and make things worse. "Yes, Bayley, but it's all the other people in Sea Breeze that I don't know I can trust. Do you know every person in there?" He waved a hand toward Sip This. "Your stalker is out there somewhere and we don't have a clue who he is or what he even…"

His words stumbled to a stop as the midmorning sun shot out of the clouds, covering her with glorious yellow light.

"Cruse?"

He didn't speak, couldn't really, caught the way he was by the deep blue of her eyes, glimmering as the trees made the sunshine dance across her face. She was so beautiful.

Cruse took one step closer to Bayley. Her brows drew together and she took a hesitant step back, one hand on her hip, uncertainty on her face. "Cruse? What's the matter with you?"

He'd like to know the same exact thing. He prided himself on being able to detach himself from the emotion of the moment on the job. Emotions were messy, and better left for later, not the middle of a crisis. But Bayley…well, all he could think was "hunh."

With no real conscious thought, Cruse closed the distance between them, tunneled his fingers into that thick golden brown mane of hers and curved them around the base of her neck.

Her eyes grew wide as she registered what he meant to do, and drifted closed as his mouth closed over hers. He slid one arm down her back to her waist and drew her closer. She tasted of coffee and peppermint.

When she wrapped her arms around his neck and pulled him even nearer, he closed his own eyes, losing himself in the joy of being with Bayley, being this close to her. She fit him perfectly. If he didn't know better, he'd have thought she'd been made for him.

He broke the kiss.

Because he did know better. Bayley Foster hadn't been made for him. They came from two different worlds. She deserved a nice man to settle down with. Someone safe, some suit-and-tie guy, who drove a nice reliable sedan, and who came home at night. Not him.

Did God *know* how difficult this was? Holding on to someone like her, and wondering why she couldn't be in the plan for his life? Because no matter how much he wanted to make that sweetness his, she didn't belong to him and never would.

He dropped his arms from around her and took a step back.

Her eyes, cloudy and dreamy, went confused. "Cruse?"

"I've got work. Stick with Sailor. Tell her to call me if anything happens." He backed toward his motorcycle as he spoke.

"Tell her…right." Bayley crossed her arms across her chest.

Cruse gunned his Harley and sped down the drive of Sip This, running from Bayley, wishing he could run as easily from the feelings she stirred up in him.

* * *

So, Cruse mused, what kind of flowers say, *I'm sorry I kissed you, can we go back to a platonic relationship?* Except if he were honest with himself, he'd admit that he didn't want to go back to friendship. In fact, maybe that wasn't ever what he'd wanted with her. Good thing he wasn't into being honest with himself.

If he'd been into honesty, he would've thought of her next to him, his ring on her finger, forever. But *forever* wasn't in his vocabulary. God had a lot more work to do in his life before he could believe that word in connection to a relationship, if ever.

He looked around the florist shop, bewildered by the choices—roses of every size and color; those other ones were carnations he thought; and then those…maybe those were funky colored daisies. He shoved his hands into his pockets. He didn't know which to get. Daisies seemed common for Bayley, not really fitting. And he was staying *way* away from roses.

"Well, hey, Cruse!" Gloria bustled in from the back. "I didn't hear the bell ring, but Jorge has that music turned up so loud back there. I don't know how the man can think, much less be the creative genius that he swears he is!" Gloria, with her bleached-blond hair piled in big loose curls on top of her head, had curves as generous as her spirit. She'd been in Cruse's class in night school when he'd moved here—one of the few who'd looked beyond his obvious poverty and been kind. "So what can I get for ya, honey?"

Cruse shrugged a shoulder, feeling way out of his league. "I need something for a friend. I don't want it to be really personal."

"Just some carnations would do for that, I'd think. Kinda unimaginative, but cheap."

"No, she's not the generic type. What else have you got?"

Gloria thought, tapping the side of her face with her pencil. "What about calla lilies? They're gorgeous, very elegant and sophisticated."

She opened the case behind her and hefted a vase out, filled with large, white, waxy blooms. They were slick, but not Bayley. He hated to dim the hopeful look on Gloria's face but, "No, those definitely aren't her either."

"Hmm. What say you tell me what she's like and I'll help you pick out some flowers?" Could she be more amused? He couldn't be more mortified.

"She's uh…" How did you describe Bayley? "She's smart and strong, but she's pretty, too. She's got a way of looking right into a person. She's really easy with herself, brave. She likes kids and dogs?" He finished with a half laugh, and another embarrassed shrug.

"I think I have the perfect thing. I'll be right back." Gloria disappeared into the back room and returned a moment later with a short ceramic pot overflowing with violets. "These aren't fancy, but they're really pretty, and they're tough, too. Tougher than they look."

"They're perfect for her. Nice pick."

"Thanks, Cruse. I did choose the right profession, didn't I?" She selected a purple ribbon the exact shade of the violets and threaded it around the neck of the decorative pot. "You know, between you and your partner, you guys are paying my overhead this week."

The back of Cruse's neck prickled. "Slay was in here buying flowers?"

"Yeah, it was a few days ago, came in and bought two dozen roses." She winked at Cruse. "And he was just about as embarrassed as you were."

"So you think he was feeling extravagant that day, or what?"

"Thoughtful, I'd say. I delivered the ones for his mom. And, let me tell you, she was tickled pink." She gave the bow a final fluff and turned to Cruse. "That'll be eighteen ninety-five."

Cruse tried for casual as he dug a twenty out of his pocket. "What color roses did Slay pick?" *Please say yellow, peach, pink, something other than...*

"Red, red, red. That man has a serious romantic streak if you ask me. And he was giving no hints about the identity of the gal getting that second dozen roses, and believe me, I hinted plenty for a clue, even told him I'd waive the delivery fee, but he wasn't talking. He took that dozen roses and kept his mouth sealed up tight." She handed Cruse his change and slid the violets a little closer. "Yeah, it's just as well you weren't buying roses. I'm down to slim pickings. Seems everybody had a need for them this week."

"Is there a way you can get me a list of everyone who bought roses and what color?"

Gloria narrowed her eyes to shrewd slits. "Would this be police business, Cruse?"

"It could be, yeah."

She turned to her computer and typed a few keys, muttering to herself. "And let me cross-reference for color..." She tapped one final key and the printer began to hum under the counter. In seconds Cruse had a complete customer list cross-matched by color and method of payment.

"Gloria, I don't know what to say."

"Don't look so dumbfounded, Conyers. The color of my hair comes from a bottle, not nature. Shoot, you don't think my business got this successful by luck, do you? I got my M.B.A. last year. You're looking at a professional business-woman."

"Full of surprises, Gloria."

"Aren't I just?" She spread the pages on the counter. "You know most of these folks. My customers tend to be locals. See, there's Mrs. Phillips. She bought a ka-jillion dozen last

Saturday—Garden Club at her house, I think. There's Mrs. Garner. She buys them to make her husband jealous. Thomas Stanfield bought a dozen reds. He's your neighbor, right?"

"Yeah, he is. Did you deliver those?"

"Nope. And he didn't say one word to me. Didn't even smile, just ordered the roses, took them and left." She made it sound like a crime. But then it probably was to someone as gregarious as Gloria.

"Do you remember anyone that made you nervous, or suspicious? Someone who would've paid with cash?"

"No, hon. I wish I did." A crash followed by a Spanish curse word sounded out of the back room.

Gloria sighed, a long-suffering lift of her shoulders. "Now I'm going to have to go talk Jorge off the ceiling." She pushed the violets across the counter to Cruse. "Don't be a stranger, Cruse Conyers."

"I'll try not to be, Gloria. See you around."

The heat hit him in the face as he walked back outside, trying to slide his sunglasses on with his one unoccupied hand, trying not to think about Slayton and what the new information might mean. He glanced down at the list. Half his neighbors could be suspects if this list was correct.

Despite the heat of the day, Cruse shivered. Gloria, in her friendly breezy way, had really messed up an already extremely rotten day.

EIGHT

Bayley eased open the door to Cruse's house, her feet throbbing. Even exhausted as she was, she couldn't help a little trepidation as she stepped inside. It wasn't going "home" to Cruse's house instead of her own, though that was strange in itself. But stalkers liked welcome-home surprises. Bayley didn't.

She could smell coffee brewing, though—that smelled like home. Dropping her shoes by the fireplace, she caught sight of flowers on the counter in the kitchen. She shivered, an involuntary reaction, and glanced around the room, making sure she was alone. Deep-purple violets, not roses, sat on the counter. A card had been placed beside the arrangement.

I thought these looked like you.

Cruse had signed his name in a dark black scrawl. He hadn't been in a pleasant mood. Despite herself, she laughed and lifted the bouquet to smell it. These flowers were from Cruse and were about friendship, not terror. A small part of what had been broken began to mend.

He'd been running when he left the coffee shop earlier. She had enough understanding of him to know that. He liked things in control, ordered, his way. He had feelings for her, and the feelings weren't simple, or easily filed. A smile curved across her face. He could try to put her in a box—exactly what he'd tried to do when he'd zoomed away on that gigantic motorcycle of his—and though the flowers were lovely, no amount of violets could make her stay where he put her.

She grabbed a bottle of water from the refrigerator—and a dog biscuit from the jar on the counter when Scruffy nosed her insistently. If she was lucky, she might have time for a quiet hour on the porch—time to reflect and pray about the things that had been happening to her at breakneck speed. Walking closer to the screen, she stopped short at the sight on the beach. Cruse wore denim cutoffs, and a ragged *SBPD* T-shirt.

He sliced the shovel into the sand and turned to a pile of wood, tossing logs into the pit. As if he sensed her watching him, he looked up at the house and crooked his finger. *Come here.*

She took her time. Her feet met the cool, silky sand, and still she lingered, watching Cruse. He reached behind him into a brown paper bag and came up with lighter fluid and matches. In a macho move, he doused the kindling and lit the logs in the pit into a gigantic beach bonfire.

He rambled back and sprawled out beside where she sat on the beach blanket, ending up propped on one elbow. The sun eased down, spreading pinkish orange light against surly summer storm clouds out in the Gulf.

"Cruse, what is all this?"

"I was rude today, and I wanted to apologize." He shrugged with one shoulder. "You said you'd never had a pep rally or a bonfire. I can't really provide the friends, but you have those of your own."

A car door slammed and the sound of laughter carried to her over the sand. Bayley turned back to Cruse, questioning.

"I called your assistant and she told me the name of your church. Your pastor's a great guy. I talked to him on the phone. He knows my pastor, so they're coming out tonight and bringing a few friends."

Her minister, Lucas Ford, trudged over the sand dune from Cruse's house with a take-out bag from the local deli. "Hi, Bayley."

"Lucas?" Her eyes stung. "You didn't have to come all the way out here. I know you're really busy."

Her pastor, with sandy-blond hair and a big smile, wrapped his free arm around her shoulders. "What's more important than spending an evening with friends?"

Another guy with a battered guitar slung over one shoulder joined them at the bonfire.

"Bayley, this is my pastor, Jake Rollins."

"Hi, Jake."

She sent Cruse a bewildered smile—that Cruse would organize this for her warmed her to her toes, and that her pastor would want to join them overwhelmed her.

Two women from the Bible study group Bayley had joined came next. Suz trudged through the sand and thunked a huge basket of food on the quilt.

Cruse actually laughed. "Hey, I bought food!"

He reached into the bag again and came out with two huge bags of marshmallows and a handful of wire coat hangers. "We'll have to wait for the fire to die down a bit, but in a little while we can roast marshmallows for s'mores."

Bayley's friend Carlianne squeezed Bayley into a huge hug. "Hey, girl. Your guy knows how to throw a party."

"Thanks so much for coming, Carli. I can't tell you how…" Her teeth snagged her bottom lip as a huge lump of emotion clogged her throat. Not that she didn't know she had friends—she had figured that she was making them—slowly. But that they would come to an impromptu party that Cruse threw together…it humbled her. "It means a lot."

Time passed so quickly, roasting hot dogs, and singing the praise songs that Bayley had come to love. In his apology, Cruse had effortlessly given her these things she'd desperately wanted—the bonfire, yes. But also the understanding that she had friends, and something new from God. The confidence to be herself with these friends.

She'd searched for so long for a love that she could depend on. Maybe it started with wanting her father's approval, like all little girls. But she had something better now. She had her *Father's* approval. And with Cruse's help, He had given her an amazing gift. He had shown her that she is worthy of being loved, not just as a possession, but as a child of God, and as a friend.

The song wound down and Jake put his guitar away. "How about those s'mores?"

Cruse tossed Jake a hanger, and began unwinding his. As twilight faded into darkness and the stars winked on one by one, he felt tension unwinding as well. There was no reason he couldn't enjoy this time with Bayley. He knew it wouldn't last, that whatever time he spent with her he'd have to take as a gift.

"How'd you know how to build a bonfire, Cruse? Did you and your family take a lot of camping trips as a kid?" Bayley thrust her coat hanger into the fire, laughing when her marshmallows caught on fire. She blew them out, her full-out abandon making him smile, even though her question sent doubt tumbling through him like a ton of rocks.

"No." He shared a look with his pastor, Jake. How to explain his childhood to Bayley. The truth would probably be best. It might hurt more for him, sort of like a bandage being ripped off, but she deserved to hear it. "I didn't have a dad to take me camping, but in the third grade, I went to the same school for about six months, sort of a rarity for me. The counselor there, Mrs. Rafferty, she got my mom to sign a form for me to have a Big Brother."

"That's so cool that she would do that for you." Carlianne smushed a s'more together and took a gigantic bite, marshmallow sliding out on her chin, making her giggle.

Cruse passed her a napkin. "Yeah. I'll never know how she got my mother to do that. Anyway, my Big Brother's name was Jake. He took me to ball games and played video games with me. And this one weekend, we went camping with three other Big Brothers and their kids. It was awesome. He taught me to build a fire and roast marshmallows."

Cruse smiled at the memory now. For a long time he hadn't wanted to think about it because what happened after had hurt so incredibly badly. But now he found he could think about those good memories from childhood and find something positive. He even remembered Jake, young and full of faith, trying to tell him about this unseen God that would take his burden and make it light. Cruse had been too full of anger, even at nine years old, to believe in something he couldn't see. But he'd prayed anyway, not really believing, because he'd wanted to make Jake happy.

Maybe God hadn't heard his prayers, but He'd heard Jake's prayers for him, prayers that God would reveal Himself to Cruse. And God had, like a soft whisper, revealed Himself a few years ago, showing him mercy and giving him this faith that believed in things unseen.

Tonight he had a chance to prove to Bayley that God didn't leave, even when times got tough.

"So do you still stay in contact with him?" Bayley'd given up on her own s'more, the chocolate bar and graham cracker lying idle in her lap.

"A few months after that trip, my mother moved us to a trailer park outside the city. She didn't leave a forwarding address with the school. I begged her to call Jake, but she wouldn't. She said he looked down on us." He looked around the circle of people, who looked at him, not with pity on their faces, but genuine interest. And something inside him shifted. What had started as a story for Bayley began to heal something in him. "It was cool, though. For a while."

The bonfire burned lower, bright red and orange embers glowing underneath, so he stuck a couple of marshmallows on the end of his own hanger. "There's an art to this, you know. I like to toast mine very slowly to get them just the right shade of golden brown. Crispy on the outside, mushy-squishy on the inside."

His pastor interrupted his lecture on marshmallow roasting. "You didn't tell them the rest of the story, Cruse."

Cruse met his friend's eyes again. Jake nodded. *You can do this.*

"What's the rest of the story?" Bayley scooted on the sand to sit next to Cruse.

He swallowed hard. "A couple of years ago, I was riding my Harley down the coast on a beautiful Sunday morning when I passed this church. Come to think of it, I'm not really sure I even knew it was a church until that day, but as I passed I saw a long line of motorcycles curling around the parking lot. I could hear their engines roaring and they sounded so…alive. You know?"

She nodded, the firelight glimmering in the deep blue of her eyes, and it was like he was talking only to Bayley.

"At the head of the line of bikes was this minister. He was laying hands on the bikers and blessing them before their ride. I don't know what it was, but I felt compelled to pull in and get in line. I couldn't drive past—couldn't *not* stop. The minister prayed for me—the minister who turned out to be my old Big Brother, Jake. I never finished my ride that day, but I dedicated my life to Christ with Jake's help. I've been on quite a ride ever since."

Bayley's eyes shimmered with unshed tears. "God planned it that way, Cruse."

"I agree, Bayley." Jake smiled, the deep dimple that had all the single women in the church baking him casseroles showing in his cheek. He picked his guitar up by the neck and stood. "I hate to leave, but I've got a breakfast meeting in the morning."

Suz hugged Bayley and made her promise to call for a lunch outing next week. She and Carlianne gathered their things and left with Bayley's pastor, leaving Bayley and Cruse staring into the fire, suddenly silent.

Cruse cleared his throat. "Sailor will be home soon. I guess I should get this stuff cleaned up." But he didn't move.

Her hand slid into his as the fire crackled. "Thanks for tonight. No one has ever done anything like this for me. I—"

He knew he was in over his head and going down for the third time, but what did he care? He cupped the back of her neck and leaned forward, placing his lips on hers. He breathed her in.

A heady mix of caramelly marshmallow, the coconut-mango shampoo he knew she favored, and something else, something that was simply Bayley.

Slowly, he became aware that his cell phone was ringing. He reached blindly for his phone at his waistband and looked at the readout. "I've got to take this." He didn't answer it, though. He stayed a breath away from her, wanting nothing more than to dive back in. To experience everything she had to offer and to show her...what?

To show her what? What it felt like to be left behind, to be third in line behind his job and his responsibility to his sister? It wasn't fair, but he had to stop this now before he couldn't. Because much more of steeping himself in Bayley and he wouldn't be able to walk away.

He grabbed his phone, making the call before turning back to Bayley. "I've got to go."

She didn't speak, just sat up and hugged her knees.

He stopped midmotion and sat back down beside her. "Your house has been cleared, honey. Do you want to go home?"

She shook her head, a brief jerk. "Not tonight."

"All right. Let me douse the fire and I'll walk you up."

For the first time in his life, going to work felt like running away. One more reason he *didn't* get involved.

Bayley contemplated getting up, but since Cruse kept the house arctic cold, she didn't really want to get out from under the covers. Not that the temperature would've mattered to him last night. He'd insisted on sleeping in a hammock under the house.

And today she needed to get her stuff together since she'd be going home. She should be glad to get back to her house, her yellow walls. Being Saturday, she could start painting her bedroom. She'd chosen a pink the color of a Gerbera daisy. It would probably clash hideously with the sunflower in the living room, but she didn't care. She needed brightness and certainly had gotten past worrying about what other people would think.

She found Cruse sitting on the bench on the screened porch, watching the sun come up. He hadn't noticed her yet.

The bruising on his face wasn't any better—if anything it bloomed more colorful. But the bruises didn't hold her attention, his expression did. He looked utterly and completely alone.

She poured a steaming mug of coffee from the pot Sailor had left. Taking it to the porch, Bayley stood behind him watching the ocean. The furl of the soft morning waves shone white in the dawning light, the swish of the waves a soft balm.

She sat next to Cruse, still not saying anything, and took his hand, wanting nothing more than to ease the unbearably sad expression on his face. He looked at their joined hands, and she waited for him to pull away, or say something, but he didn't. He laid his head back on the bench and his eyes drifted shut.

After two or three long minutes, Cruse opened his eyes and looked at Bayley. "Take your time, but whenever you're ready, I'll walk you home."

"Okay." What should have brought her joy and relief felt a little more like…regret?

He shifted in his chair, and eased his hand out from hers. "With your security system and Scruffy, you'll be safe. I'll tell the other cops to step up their drive-bys overnight, too."

She didn't speak, and he shifted again. He'd really changed tune since the first night her stalker struck. That night he slept on the porch. Today he couldn't wait to get rid of her.

Bayley went into Cruse's guest room, nursing not only her quickly cooling cup of coffee, but hurt feelings that she refused to give in to. Common sense said that Cruse wasn't pushing her away because he didn't like her, but because he did. But common sense saying it and her heart believing it were two different matters.

She lifted her overnight bag from the floor of the closet where she'd slung it two nights earlier and tossed it on the bed. Her colorful T-shirts were jumbled in a pile on the chair. She picked those up and tumbled them into the bag to be sorted later.

Her makeup went with one swipe of the bathroom counter into her bag and she was pretty much packed. She was still dressed in her linen pants from the night before, so she ran a brush through her hair, pulled it back into a low, smooth ponytail, and she was ready to go.

Cruse—fully dressed in his casual uniform of black jeans and T-shirt, badge and gun attached to his waistband—waited by the front door, the dog waiting not so patiently beside him. Cruse opened the front door and she swept through, not about to let him see how very much she hated to leave.

* * *

Following Bayley up the steps to her back door, Cruse had to keep himself from pulling her back and telling her he didn't mean it. He wanted her to stay at his house, but nothing good would come out of her staying with him. Nothing except the two of them in close proximity and, after yesterday, he wasn't trusting himself within ten feet of her.

Sweetness shone out of her. She made everyone she met feel important. She had to have bad traits, too. Everyone did, right? But all Cruse could come up with was her stubborn streak. Yeah, it was a mile wide, but he even had to admire that. She'd withstood a nightmare that would have broken most people.

And at the moment, she wasn't speaking to him, which he guessed was all for the best, but made him feel altogether worse than he could remember. Maybe as bad as he felt when he skinned his entire body from elbow to ankle in a bike wreck at age seven.

When Bayley reached the door, she dropped her duffel bag at her feet and reached into her purse for the key. But when she went to put the key in the lock, the door drifted open. She froze, staring at it, before she turned to look at Cruse, eyes wide.

He waved her away from the door, already with his cell phone at his ear. Somebody's head was going to roll over this one. He'd been the last one to leave here last night. CSU assured him they were finished processing the scene, and when the final carpenter left after fixing the window, Cruse himself had set the alarm.

When the CSU commanding officer answered, Cruse hit her with both barrels blazing. "This is Cruse Conyers. I'm at Bayley Foster's house and some bozo left the door unlocked and didn't reset the alarm. I want to know who the last person was out of here."

Maria Fuentes's voice was ice. "Cruse, we were through with that scene and left the property while you were still there. Whoever it was, it wasn't us. I personally had the new alarm code, but no one else in this unit did."

Cruse walked to the edge of the outer deck and looked down on the sand dunes below, leaning on one arm. He sighed. "I'm sorry, Maria. When I got here and the door was open, I jumped on the first conclusion I came to."

Fuentes sniffed in his ear. "Whatever, Cruse. Don't let it happen again." As he held the phone out to hang it up, he thought he heard her say, "Stupid detectives."

Bayley waited quietly, leaning against the house beside the open door. She knew better than to go in, he guessed.

He released Scruffy and held his weapon ready as he pushed the door to the house all the way back. He stepped into the house, eyes constantly moving, checking each area for a threat before dismissing it in his mind.

He motioned to Bayley to stay near the door when she stepped inside to survey the damage, and then he moved quickly to the outside of her bedroom. The door, slightly ajar, had not been in that position when he left yesterday.

Cruse narrowed his eyes. A faint sound drifted from the bedroom. Could someone still be in there? He braced his gun, shoved open the door and rushed the room, all in a single economical motion, the shepherd-mix dog glued to his side.

Clear.

He cleared the master bathroom before stopping to take a longer look. His lip curled, almost on its own, as he realized the bedcovers were tossed back in a heap and the pillows were piled like someone had reclined on them. Toby Keith sang from the clock radio beside Bayley's bed—the noise he'd heard.

Cruse checked the bathroom. Even weirder than the bed was the pink disposable razor, clearly one of Bayley's, that sat by the sink. Thick black whiskers remained on the blades and in the sink. Sick.

One certainty appeared in Cruse's mind. He was going to have to do some fast talking to make up with Fuentes, because her CSU team had some work in store.

Bayley stood in her living room taking in the mess. The new brightly colored pillows she had bought were rags on the floor, stuffing hanging out everywhere. A sheen of tears was in her eyes, but she didn't blink, probably willing them to go away.

Crime, bad guys, mayhem—those were topics he was comfortable with. Tears from this strong woman…well, enough said. "Bayley, I hate for you to have to do this, but can you look around and see if anything is missing? Chances are there's something, but it may be unimportant, something you wouldn't miss if you didn't look."

She nodded and began wandering around the house, her hands firmly clasped behind her back. She'd been trained well. What a shame that she had to be intimately aware of crime-scene etiquette.

Cruse resolved himself to the inevitable and redialed Fuentes's number, walking to the window as he talked.

Bayley took her time trying to picture in her mind the details of how she left the house. Some things would have been moved by the crime-scene processors the day before, and probably moved again as they were cleaned. Something out of place could be normal—missing was not.

She stepped into the bedroom and froze. Goose bumps prickled her skin. Someone had been in her bed.

Nausea boiled up in her stomach, and she gagged. Unbelievably, she wanted nothing more than to turn and run home to her parents.

Instead of retreating, she made herself take one step into

the room and then another until she stood in front of the dresser. Weaving her fingers tightly together, she clenched them so she wouldn't forget and reach out. She'd left jewelry in a tangle on the glass top of the dresser—it was still there.

Something crunched under her foot. A heavy gold bracelet or anklet glimmered in the thick carpet. She didn't touch it, but it didn't look like hers. Familiar somehow. She needed to mention it to Cruse, to be sure. As she walked forward, she caught her hip on a dresser drawer, not pushed in all the way.

A shudder racked her. She'd thought that she was used to being a victim, that she'd overcome the feeling of powerlessness that came with it, parcel and package. But the thought of some perverted person in her most personal things…she felt violated.

Bayley took slow steps to the bathroom. And had to slap her hand over her mouth to prevent the cry. Whoever had been in her house had used her razor. And left whiskers in the sink.

Panic clawed its way free. Her breath whistled in. She couldn't seem to get enough air…more…air. The strident breaths she took didn't seem to help at all and around the edges of her vision, she began to see spots.

Large hands grasped her shoulders and she gasped, struggling for a long minute before Cruse's voice sank in. "Hush, baby, it's just Cruse."

He turned her into his body and wrapped his muscular arms around her. She buried her face in his chest and allowed him to enclose her completely. She took a breath, held it to the count of ten, and blew out. And again.

Cruse murmured against her head, but she couldn't tell what he said. It didn't matter—the rumble of his voice soothed the fear and dread that had scrabbled its way to purchase.

"Come on, let's get out of here. We don't have to be inside."

He led her through the front room and outside into the fresh air. The heat, an energy-sapping danger at times, wrapped around her like a balm. She shivered as Cruse pulled her onto the porch swing, snug up next to his body.

The hard planes of his muscles reminded her of his power as a cop, but his hand on her hair, so gentle, proved that there was so much more to the man.

He'd been so patient with her, so present. Guilt nipped at her. "I'm sorry to be a burden to you, Cruse. I know my problems have been stealing time from your real work."

The cell phone chirped at his waist, and without moving her, he unclipped it from his waist. "Conyers."

Bayley felt his muscles harden and grow still as he listened. His face serious—his eyes narrowed into green slits as he scanned the ocean below them.

"Are you sure?" A long moment. "Yeah. I'll follow up. Thanks."

He flipped the phone closed and stared at it. "Bayley, do you know where Thomas is?"

She sat back and thought. "No, I don't think he's been here the past couple of days, but I don't keep tabs on him. And I've been at your house. Why?"

"That was one of our officers on the phone. The court order came through—the law firm had to release the name of the company behind the waterfront development we've been looking into regarding the S.O.S. case." Cruse took a deep breath and pulled her closer again, holding on to her as if to keep her in place. "It's Stanfield Development. Thomas's name is all over the paperwork."

NINE

"Thomas is not a murderer, Cruse."

Cruse almost hoped she was wrong. At least then he could close the stinking case. Bayley looked up to meet his eyes as she spoke, but didn't pull away from him in the swing. Maybe a sign that she had grown to trust him?

What would it cost that trust if Cruse had to bring Thomas in? He wouldn't be able to keep it from her. He wouldn't want to. Whatever happened, *he* had to trust God through this. He wanted to say that he wouldn't let himself get involved, but it was too late for that.

"I need to talk to Thomas, Bayley. He can clarify some things for us. He's by no means our only suspect."

Bayley looked back at the ocean, but her eyes didn't focus. Looking not seeing. Sometimes life was like that. As a cop, Cruse had seen more than a few families collapse when the foundation they had always believed in crumbled, as lies and deceit found their way to the light.

"Who else?"

"Let's just say that your friend isn't the only one ever crossed by S.O.S. But, honey, he has a powerful motive. I'd be negligent if I didn't pursue it."

"I'm not asking you not to pursue it. Thomas was out of

the country, in Europe, when the murders happened. He'll have a solid alibi."

For Bayley's sake, Cruse hoped so. For his own sake, he hoped he didn't have to be the one to tell her different. And of course, there was the whole murder-for-hire angle. Thomas didn't have to be the one pulling the trigger.

"Who heads Stanfield Development? Is it Thomas?"

"No, Thomas's dad is still very much in charge of that company. Thomas tries, but he's got some big shoes to fill following Mr. Stanfield."

A car door slammed downstairs. Please let it be the crime scene unit. She'd had about all she could take of this place.

Maria Fuentes grabbed her kit from the trunk of the car and hustled to where they stood at the edge of the deck, her long stride making her look more in control than a one-hundred-pound female should. "What happened here?"

The grooves around Cruse's mouth, already grim, deepened. "Someone's been in Bayley's house."

Fuentes grunted and reached down to give Scruff a scratch behind the ears, the act making the formidable woman seem somehow more agreeable. "Miss Foster, it's my professional opinion that you should get as far away from here as possible. My team and I will let you know as soon as we have any results. We'll find something, I promise you. It's my scene now."

Cruse tensed, but finally nodded. Bayley allowed him to lead her away from her house, and her car. She could almost feel all her hard-won independence circling the drain. But somehow with everything that had happened she couldn't even work up the emotion to care.

While she stared out the window of the Jeep at Fuentes, who snapped pictures of her house with quick efficient movements, Cruse buckled her into her seat belt. He touched her shoulder. "Bayley? You okay?"

Bayley jerked. "I'm fine, Cruse."

Troubled green eyes met hers, and before her eyes, his demeanor changed. She saw the shift, from friend to police detective. And his words echoed it. "This is escalating faster than anyone could've expected."

That sucking noise she heard was the very last of her so-called life going down the drain. She shrugged, taking a last look at her beach house, the same home that she'd taken so much joy in making her own.

Now she just felt defeated. "I should probably take a real leave of absence from work. I don't have anything major except the benefit tomorrow night, which I'm not calling off. But there's no way to be safe at work unless I were to call in a whole team of bodyguards, and I'm not prepared to do that. And more important than my safety, is the safety of my clients at the shelter. They don't deserve this."

She wanted him to touch her, to hold her hand, but when she looked at him, all she saw was the cop. She looked away.

"Bayley."

She continued her stare at the turmoil of the waves on the beach. They mirrored her inner turmoil.

"Bayley, I promise, we're going to find the guy and then this *will* be over."

Tears welled up in her eyes. She blinked them back. She'd made this decision and wouldn't cry over it. Not now.

Cruse said, "I've got to go to work for a while. Will you come with me?"

"I guess." It wasn't like she had anything else to do right now. "I don't want to be a burden, Cruse. All I wanted to do here is be self-sufficient. I don't want to need anyone. I'm too much. This is all just too much."

"We always need God, Bay. And sometimes God sends other people to be His helping hands. There's no shame in taking it. I learned that with Jake. Where would I be if he hadn't given his time for me?"

Cruse led the way into the three-story, gray, metal building. "My office is on the third floor."

Inside, when Cruse opened the door to the stairwell, Bayley put on the brakes. "Oh, no. I can't handle three flights of stairs after the day I've had. There's got to be an elevator here somewhere."

Cruse shifted his weight and tried to draw her into the stairwell. "There is. But I always take the stairs."

Bayley shook her head, literally drooping at the thought of climbing all those stairs. She tilted her head back and squinted to see straight up to the top. There were, like, a million of them. "Please, Cruse?"

Inexplicable reluctance written all over Cruse's face, he led her to the elevator and stepped on behind her with the dog.

Bayley sank against the back wall. She truly was exhausted. When she thought back to all the emotional hits she'd taken today, it was no wonder she wanted to find the nearest comfortable chair and collapse.

On the other hand, Cruse had to be in a hurry to get to work because he was as jumpy as she'd ever seen him. He paced back and forth in front of the door of the elevator as it climbed, pausing to brace his hands, one on either side of the door.

When the bell rang and the doors opened, Cruse barreled through the doors and into the reception area of the detectives' offices. Slayton Cross stood next to the receptionist's desk reading pink message slips.

Cruse pushed past him, too, straight to the water dispenser. He poured a cup of water, downed it and poured again. Slayton looked at Bayley with a half-amused look. "Impressive—you can even get him to follow you on elevators."

Slayton's sarcastic remark took Bayley by surprise, but she focused on Cruse and let it slide. Cruse's complexion faded to gray, his breathing rapid, and as she watched, he swiped a forearm across a sweaty forehead.

When she turned back to Slayton with dawning comprehension, he shrugged. "As long as I've known him, he's always taken the stairs."

Wow. Claustrophobia? It must be, or something close. Okay, so the stubborn man preferred an anxiety attack to being honest with her. What should that tell her?

She crossed to Cruse, who crumpled his paper cup and threw it in the trash can. Just for a minute, when she met his eyes, she could see the uncertainty, the need for understanding, before he shuttered it with his cop face. "You could have told me."

"Told you what, Bayley?"

She narrowed her eyes. "I thought we were beyond cop and victim. I thought we were friends, too."

Cruse took an actual step back, the wall he'd built earlier, the one she recognized as the cop wall, firmly in place. Her friend was gone; she'd already lost him.

"I can't talk about this right now," he muttered, motioning toward a door somewhere in the vicinity behind him. "You can stay in the break room while I get some work done."

An hour later, Bayley sat at the table in the break room, an extremely bad cup of precinct coffee in front of her, flipping through "Manly Man" magazine, or whatever its real name was. That article about guerilla warfare in urban police work couldn't be more fascinating.

A change in the room's barometric pressure made Bayley look up. She turned toward the door to find Cruse lounging against the door frame. His color was better, but his expression was anything but.

Bayley motioned to the chair across the table from her, and Cruse sat down heavily, the dog settling at his feet. "Are you all right?"

His expression went from sour to blank in an instant. "I'm fine."

Well, she could guess what he *didn't* want to talk about.

Then he sighed, turning his hands up on his lap in a gesture of surrender. "These cases are getting to me. First, we have your stalker situation. We've got evidence out the wazoo and no one to tie it to. Then there's the S.O.S. cases. We have speculation, but zero evidence tying any particular person to the murders. Everywhere I turn I run into a brick wall. I guess I'm stubborn enough to keep banging my head against it until something cracks, but I'm not enjoying it."

Regret reared its conscientious head. Yes, Cruse was avoiding any conversation about what happened in the elevator earlier, but she had no doubt he was being honest with her now. Of course he'd take the lack of progress personally. That's who he was. "I'm sorry, Cruse. Can I help with anything?"

Cruse threw out a humorless laugh. "Get Charles Stanfield to give me an appointment?"

Bayley flipped the magazine closed and dropped it on the table. "That I can do. I may not be able to get you in his office, but I can definitely get you in his presence. The rest would be up to you."

"How?"

Bayley lifted a shoulder, and an eyebrow. "I've got that fund-raising event tomorrow night. My parents, the Stanfields, they'll all be there. You can come as my escort, but you'll need a tux."

Cruse was already on his feet. "Let's go shopping."

He took two steps toward the door with her and stopped, his cop face dropping just for a second. "Bayley—thanks."

She nodded, wishing for the millionth time she could get beneath that detective shell to the heart of who Cruse really was. He'd share glimpses, like at the bonfire the other night, just enough to fool her into thinking they might actually be friends. But she knew better. He shared too much resemblance to every other protector she'd ever had. And he'd walk away just like they did.

Maybe this time she should be the one doing the walking.

After buying Cruse's tux, Bayley needed some time to tie up loose ends at the office. Cruse needed time to think. His every instinct said he was on the right track. *Find the motive, find the stalker.* Scott Fallon didn't commit the latest crimes against Bayley. He had nothing to gain and everything to lose.

Cruse accelerated as the light turned green. So who could be doing this to Bayley?

Slayton. He—possibly—had a past with her that he kept hidden. He bought roses. He had the ability to get inside information, and he definitely had the brains to pull off the crimes. But why would he?

He didn't want to believe it was Slayton. Could Cruse possibly have worked with him all this time and not picked up on that part of his personality? No way.

Another possibility was Thomas. Thomas had opportunity, and he probably knew the contents of the note, but again, what motive? He'd been closer to Bayley than anyone besides her own family.

Maybe one of the abusive men whose wife Bayley sheltered. Maybe someone who had a beef with her father. Or maybe she'd cut some vindictive society chick.

And maybe Cruse had missed something vital that would have kept Bayley out of danger.

You don't have to do it on your own. The thought sprang to mind, and Cruse knew he didn't put it there. He looked up, knowing his faith was growing, trust was growing, and that voice in his heart reminded him what he'd been through in his own life.

"So what's the plan, God? How do we not let Bayley be

another Sailor? Another person I let down?" And then his heart twisted. "And when this is over, how do I walk away from her?"

Reluctantly, he turned his mind from Bayley to the S.O.S. case. With any luck, he'd get a lead from Stanfield at the benefit. Cruse hoped he could get a lead, because all this circling around the same information was gaining him nothing but dead ends.

Cruse picked Bayley up at the shelter and drove along Bayfront Parkway to get back to the beach. The late afternoon sun sparkled on the water of Pensacola Bay like tiny diamonds.

Bayley sighed. "Even in the middle of all this trouble, I can't help but think this place is so incredibly beautiful."

Without thinking, Cruse replied, "Yeah, sometimes looking at it, you wouldn't even guess the kind of hellholes that exist in this city."

A sharp glance from Bayley had him thinking, *uh-oh*. "I mean, all cities have bad parts, right?"

She let it go, but he could see her mind working and knew he had to tell her now, so she would understand why a real relationship would never work for them. He'd hurt her this morning, pushing her away. He knew it, even though she hadn't said anything.

"I grew up here, Bayley." He pulled off the road into a parking area so he could give her his full attention. "In one of those places I was talking about. My mother was a drunk, my father…I don't even know who he was. To be truthful, I'm pretty sure he was someone my mother slept with to get money for her next drink. Even our names were throwaways. She 'thinks' we were fathered by sailors from the navy base."

Bayley put a hand on his arm. "Cruse, you don't have to do this. I don't care where you grew up or what your family was like." She looked at him with those deep, liquid-blue eyes of hers and he wanted to cave. But if he didn't tell her now, he might never.

He threw the Jeep in gear, driving as fast as he dared. In just a few minutes—unbelievable that a few minutes could make the difference between Bayley's waterfront neighborhood and his own—they pulled up in front of a dilapidated row of narrow wood-sided houses. Places that had years before been built for factory workers, that had fallen into such deep disrepair that they now were condemned. Construction equipment lined the inner courtyard, long bare of grass or any healthy growing thing.

"That's where I lived, Bayley." Cruse pointed to a sagging building at the end of the row. The one that maybe had once been a soft green color, but had been the color of bile for as long as he could remember. "That awesome place is my childhood home."

He saw the shock in Bayley's expression as she took in the sagging shutters and peeling paint. Who could blame her?

She'd grown up in that insulated world of wealth. As a kid here, she'd have had no reason to know places like this— where hopelessness hung heavy in the air—even existed.

To his surprise, when the shock faded, it wasn't revulsion that he saw. She spoke in hushed tones. "Cruse, I want to know you. If you need to tell me this, I'll listen. But it won't change how I feel about you, about the man that you are."

He opened the door of his Jeep and got out. The front entrance was boarded up with crisscrossed two-by-fours, but Cruse jerked them off. When he'd uncovered the door, he kicked it open, knocking it against the wall it hung on.

Bayley followed him into the dump he grew up in, her throat aching with unshed tears for the little boy who had lived here. Dust drifted in the air, swirling almost like smoke in the dark living room. Weak sunlight filtered through the dirty windows.

Bayley stepped in behind Cruse. His back was to her and he stood so still, she didn't know if he even realized she was there. But then he spoke.

"I got beat from the time I was old enough to use the bathroom." He crossed, step by slow, careful step, to the bedroom door. "She used to lock me in that closet when I was bad, or when she wanted me out of the way for a while. I still have claustrophobia. The elevator...I can't stand to be in any small, dark place."

He looked at her, all the anguish in his voice apparent on his face. She reached for him, but he took a step back.

"She's still there, inside me, Bayley. Don't you get that?"

Bayley swiped at her cheeks with the palms of her hands.

Cruse didn't speak for a moment, but looked at the gouges in the floor where a bed had stood. "I was out of high school, working for the police department, taking classes at the college, crashing on friends' floors most of the time. I went home for a change of clothes."

He didn't move or look at her, lost in his memories. "When I walked in the front door, I knew something wasn't right. Later I thought I might have heard Sailor whimper, but I don't know if that was real."

Suddenly Bayley didn't want to know. She didn't want to know what happened that long-ago afternoon. The hair on the back of her neck bristled. "Cruse..."

"I walked, kind of sneaked, really, to the bedroom door and caught him—the jerk my mother was dating—with my sister. I'll never forget the look on her face when she saw me. I didn't protect her." His voice was hoarse. "I didn't protect my own sister."

"Oh, Cruse. It wasn't your fault." A sob caught in Bayley's throat.

"I pulled him off her and punched him a few times, at first because I wanted to, then because I couldn't stop. I pushed him out of our house, and threw his clothes out in the yard behind him. Then I had to go in there and help my sister stand up. She couldn't even stand on her own.

"When my mother came home, we told her what he did to Sailor, but she wouldn't believe us. She actually looked her bruised and battered daughter in the eye and told her to get out. We left that night, me and Sailor."

He looked around, dazed, as if only now realizing where he was. "I haven't seen this place—or my mother—since."

"Cruse." She said it again so he would look at her. "Cruse. I was wrong when I told you that whatever you told me wouldn't change how I felt about you."

Despair shot through him so fast, it rocked him on his heels. He stayed on his feet, but inside he crumbled. He'd expected that Bayley wouldn't feel the same, but he hadn't expected her to come right out and say it. He'd had to tell her because she couldn't decide about him unless she knew it all.

And now she knew it, the whole sordid story of Cruse Conyers. And she could walk away for herself. No pushing required.

TEN

"Cruse, I never imagined what you had to do to make yourself into the man that you are today. You are…amazing."

A different kind of pain speared through him. The kind of pain caused by wanting something you couldn't have. As a kid, he'd wanted a mom like other kids had. A mom that fixed cuts and bruises with a Band-Aid, a mom that made cookies and came to baseball games. After a while, he'd learned that the wanting just made the hurt worse. So he'd trained himself not to want. Not to dream.

"Bayley, we've really got to talk."

She grabbed for his hands. "I want to go first," she said, and he held his tongue, biding his time until he could make her understand why they were so wrong for each other.

"I can't tell you how much I respect you, what you've made of yourself. It takes someone incredibly strong and principled to overcome what you have. And to choose to make a difference in other people's lives where you couldn't in your own. I'm *proud* to know you."

His battered heart couldn't take much more. He closed his eyes. "You see something in me that isn't there, Bay."

When he opened his eyes, she was already shaking her head. "No, you're wrong. I see what you can't see."

Her simple faith shamed him. "Bayley…"

The ring of his cell phone startled them both. Cruse dropped her hands, clenching his into fists, before snatching the phone from his waist.

Bayley was beginning to hate Cruse's phone. At the very least, it meant he'd probably be leaving her. He checked the readout and answered the call, his voice curt and low. Bayley's stomach tightened. *Please, no more. Not today.*

"We've got to head for the hospital." His mouth tightened into a grim line. "It's Bo Wexler. He was here in Pensacola for a court appearance Monday. He's been beaten. They say he's conscious, but are not sure for how long."

A few minutes later, when Cruse parked in the loading zone, Bayley balked. She didn't want to go in, to see a man she'd liked lying there with tubes, struggling to talk. "I'll wait here."

Cruse stopped halfway to the door and turned back, his eyes darkening with compassion. "Bay, I know a hospital is the last place you want to be, but it's not safe for you to stay in the car. You can wait outside the room if you don't want to see him."

She swung her feet out of the Jeep. Cruse was there, holding her hand as she slid down to the ground. "Let's go."

At the information desk, once Cruse had shown credentials, the volunteers told him that Wexler had been moved to prep for surgery. They'd better hurry if they wanted to catch him.

Cruse tightened his grasp on Bayley's hand and ran down the hall to the elevator. Without speaking, they turned as one and hit the stairwell to the third floor.

Cruse slammed the big silver button to open the doors to surgery, coming to a skidding stop in front of the nurses' desk. He flashed his credentials again and the nurse pointed him to a holding room.

Bayley didn't know if she wanted to go in. Cruse went

ahead of her into the room, but she stalled. So much had happened today. The attack at her house, the revelations by Cruse. She still had to process it all.

She could so see why Cruse chose to be a cop, protecting people. He had—when many people *wouldn't have*—chosen the path that led to rules and control after the chaos of his childhood, and the attack on his sister had only hardened his resolve to protect those weaker.

And that was what she was to Cruse—someone weaker to be protected. Just like all her other bodyguards. This time it had felt different, but maybe she'd been lying to herself.

She wasn't lying to herself now. She was not some weak chick that couldn't handle the sight of blood. And she might pick up on something Cruse missed.

She stepped quietly through the door of the room and had to stifle a gasp of dismay. Bo lay on the gurney, but she wouldn't have known it was him. His face was swollen beyond recognition. Purple and red bruises marked his arms and radiated from his chest over his collar bone, which protruded from the skin. She whispered a prayer. *Oh, God, please help him heal.*

Bayley walked around to the other side of the bed where she could lean over Bo and hear the breathy words he forced out. His eyes were closed, so swollen she didn't know if he even could open them. She slid her hand under his misshapen one, understanding from experience that he was scared—waiting for surgery, no family, no friends, and the ever-present fear of death lurking close. The difference was she'd had family, and she'd had faith. She prayed that Bo had at least that little bit of comfort.

He whispered and Cruse leaned close. "Two men. Bats. Faces covered, but…" His voice trailed off and Bayley thought he'd lost consciousness, but his tongue crept out to moisten cracked and bleeding lips.

"…saw a chain. Big gold chain. Peace sign. Stupid."

She heard Cruse's quick gasp, just as Bo Wexler's breath rasped in—strident, urgent. He arched his back, machines shrieking alarm. The next second, nurses and doctors had swarmed around the bed, checking the machines, his vitals, were bagging him and rolling him toward surgery. The one Cruse had spoken to at the desk called back, "Hope you got your questions answered. He's not going to be talking again for a long, long time."

Bayley stood still against the wall, where she'd been pushed when the frenzy of activity started. The room was as suddenly empty as it had been filled with activity just seconds earlier. No bed, no shrieking machines, no living patient. Just wires hanging where they'd been left and a lone latex glove that someone had dropped. The whole place seemed weirdly silent.

Cruse's deeply troubled gaze met hers and he held out a hand. Silently, they bowed their heads and prayed for the man that they both liked. As she closed her prayer, the thought that the day could not get any worse started to weave its way through her admittedly exhausted mind. She stopped it right there. Because in this crazy, mixed-up world, one thing she could definitely count on was more trouble.

Cruse pulled into his driveway and sat with his eyes closed, head leaned back against the headrest. He heard Bayley shift and rolled his head to the side so he could look at her. Exhaustion was evident in the fine lines of fatigue on her face. "I don't want you to be alone tonight."

"That's good because I don't want to be alone." She slid out of the Jeep onto the shell driveway. "I also don't want to be inside. Can we walk?"

She tuned in to him so easily it was scary. How did she know? How could she possibly sense that tonight was one of those nights where even the walls of his house would close him in, make him feel like a caged animal?

He grabbed his big flashlight out of the floorboard of the backseat, rounded the Jeep and linked his fingers with hers. Together, they crossed under his house to the beach. Kicking off her shoes, Bayley kept pace with him stride for stride through the soft sand that led to the waterfront. The ocean matched his mood tonight, rough and a little surly.

That meeting with Bo Wexler had shaken him. He needed time to think about it, but one thing was obvious. The men who attacked Bo were the same men who beat Cruse up outside the bar. The implications of that suddenly became clear. He hadn't been investigating S.O.S. that night. He'd been asking questions about Bayley's stalker.

Did that mean that Bayley's stalker and the S.O.S. case were somehow linked? He couldn't see how those two seemingly unrelated cases could possibly intertwine. But he knew at least one thing…he wasn't letting Bayley out of his sight until he figured this out because nothing was more important than keeping her safe. This woman's growing importance in his life shifted the ground under his feet faster than any wave stole sand in the pulling tide.

Thunder rolled in the distance, adding fuel to his unease. The breeze off the ocean, while still there, gusted heavy and humid. Storms brewed offshore, no doubt.

They walked steadily, putting distance between them and Cruse's house and Bayley's. Bayley seemed to need the open spaces as much as he did, but she was quiet.

Lightning streaked across the sky. Bayley gasped and for the first time, her footsteps faltered. "We need to go back."

He was already pulling her with him, breaking into a run. He'd let his attention wander. He'd been so focused on their current situation that he'd forgotten other dangers lurked besides bad guys with baseball bats.

Deafening thunder crashed simultaneously with a pop of electricity. He hit the beach, rolled and jerked Bayley back to her feet. Too late to get home, they needed shelter fast. A lifeguard stand about a hundred feet away would do. He pointed to it, yelling over the thunder that rolled again. Cruse sprinted up the steps. The door, of course, was locked.

He kicked it. It buckled, but didn't give. His bare foot hit it again just under the doorknob and it slammed open. Pulling Bayley in, he shoved the door shut against the fierce wind trying to whip it out of his hands.

"Whoa." Bayley laughed, shaky hands pushing damp, wildly tangled strands of hair back from her face. "That was close."

Cruse paced the eight-foot-square box, dark except for the crack of brighter darkness showing from outside. His flashlight had gone out in the wild roll across the sand, but he flicked it back on and slapped it in his hands a couple of times. Weak, but there, it flickered to life.

Bayley stood still, her arms wrapped around her midriff, shaking, even though the air in here was muggy hot. Cruse looked around the tiny space and found a stack of beach towels and some rescue floats that the lifeguards used. "We might as well try to find a way to be comfortable. This thing could blow through in ten minutes or it could be a line of storms that lasts all night."

He leaned the floats against the wall and covered the plywood floor with a thick layer of towels. Sitting on the floor against the floats, he stretched his legs out in front of him. He wasn't going to think about being trapped in this small space.

He wouldn't. He was in no danger. In fact, this small space was a haven. He needed to focus on Bayley, anything but the breath-stealing closeness of this tiny, dark box, too much like the closet his mother had locked him in. *Was* there enough air in here?

Bayley knelt beside him, facing him, bringing her scent with her—a little ocean wildness, a little of her coconut-mango shampoo. He breathed her in.

Too late, Cruse realized that being close to Bayley overwhelmed him every bit as much as his claustrophobia, bringing up old desires. New ones, too, desires that had nothing to do with the physical and everything to do with the future. A future that he could have no part in, not with her.

"You okay?" Cruse needed to hear Bayley say it.

Electricity crackled in the air, the small building swaying slightly in the buffeting wind. His muscles tensed as he held himself still.

She shivered again. "Yes, I'm not afraid. Not with you."

Her husky voice wrapped around him in the darkness, laced with the fine tremor of the aftermath of adrenaline. He knew it, recognized it for what it was. He'd felt it often enough.

"I'm glad." He wanted to touch her, to feel for himself that she was in one piece.

"You know, the pastor of my parents' church told me after I was stabbed that God doesn't give us more than we can handle."

Cruse paused, not wanting to misstep, not when she'd been so hurt. "I don't believe it says that anywhere in the Bible. I'm no Bible scholar, Bayley, but look at Paul—he was shipwrecked, beaten, put in prison. And more than once. I think that would be more than anyone could handle."

She shifted to rest up against him in the dark narrow space. "More than anyone could handle *on his own*."

"Yes, I'm pretty sure that's what God promises. Not that bad things won't happen, but that He'll be there with us when they do. And that's what I had to learn—that I wasn't going through life on my own. Just my meeting Jake again proves that."

Cruse slid his arm around the base of her neck, coming to an abrupt stop as he felt smooth skin knob and pucker. Her scar. The wound that stalker Scott Fallon had put there with a knife.

Cruse's hand shook as he slid it around to close on her shoulder. He could so easily have lost her before he even had known her. Another few inches...

His thumb rubbed circles over the nubby scar, to show her the feel of it didn't matter, but he didn't know if she was self-conscious, if somehow his touching her there would bring back those awful memories.

She pulled back, away from him.

"No, wait, Bay." The last thing he wanted her to think was that *she* was somehow scarred, somehow not attractive, when that was the furthest thing from the truth. "I—"

"Stop worrying, Cruse. I'm not embarrassed by it. It reminds me to take what I can from life, to enjoy every minute. Even this."

Cruse lifted his other hand to cup Bayley's cheek, drawing her close. There was such joy in this woman, and a beauty that had nothing to do with her outer figure.

"Bayley," he breathed. "You are so beautiful."

He leaned closer, then closed his mouth over hers.

And as emotion poured through him, he realized he'd made a serious error in judgment. Suddenly, the close confines of the lifeguard shack didn't matter, because now he had a new fear. Now that he'd held Bayley close, how could he possibly let her go again?

Bayley drew a sharp breath. As the furious storm whipped against the outside of their tiny shelter, it had nothing on the storm raging inside her. She shook, shivering despite the muggy closeness of the lifeguard shack. Cruse pulled his outer shirt off, leaving his T-shirt. Damp as it was, he draped it around her shoulders. Always thinking of her, always protecting her. Why then did he seem to always come two steps forward and take three steps back? Why did he put up walls that would rival the Great Wall of China when she got too close?

The storm spent itself as suddenly as it came. Rain tap-tapped on the roof, making the tiny room feel like a cocoon. Her hair hung around her face. Cruse tugged a strand that stuck to her cheek and tucked it behind her ear.

She followed him when he pushed to his feet, opened the door and stepped out into the rain. "Why do you do this, Cruse?"

He turned to face her on the outside steps of the lifeguard stand, and Bayley moved to stand a step above him, her mouth even with his. Soft, unhurried rain pattered down around him, bathing his face and shoulders.

His voice was low, almost lazy, as he asked, "Do what, Bayley?"

"Spend time with me, protecting me, even though you don't want to? I can tell sometimes that being with me is the last place you want to be."

He slid an arm around her waist and pulled her snug against his body, kissing her again, making her knees weaken and her pulse jump. "For you. You've been afraid long enough."

He let go of her, stepped down to the bottom step and looked back at her, his eyes dark and unreadable in the cloudy night. "And for me. Because I'm so selfish I want to keep you beside me as long as I can."

"You're not selfish, Cruse."

The corner of his mouth kicked up in a half smile. She could tell he didn't believe her, but he'd decided to humor her. Meeting him on the bottom step, she slung her arm around his waist and drew him down the beach toward his house—a house that, garage-sale furniture and all, with Cruse in it, felt more like a home than any she'd ever had.

Bayley's gala benefit evening was crystal clear. Not a cloud in the sky. Even the usual build of late afternoon heat was missing, a cool breeze off the water making the outdoors as appealing as the indoors. Which was nice because even though Bayley's parents' house was huge, one hundred and fifty guests craving air-conditioning would have been more than Cruse's claustrophobic self could handle.

He stood on the back deck, an old-fashioned marble portico that stretched over a long sloping backyard. The softly lapping water of Bayou Texar, at the base of the yard, glowed in the evening light. In the crowd, he could pick out the police officers, but only because he knew who they were. They were there to keep an eye on Bayley, along with the extra security that she said her father always hired during an event. She stood on the lawn in the middle of a group, graceful in a sleeveless butter-yellow dress.

He didn't want to think about Bayley, the impossible closeness he'd felt to her in that lifeguard stand last night, not here. But looking at her now, her hair in an elegant twist, long legs tipped with high heels, he couldn't help but think of the dichotomy of his beach girl—wildly beautiful last night like the ocean he loved, coolly sophisticated tonight. So many moods, so many faces. An almost irresistible combination, but one rife with complications.

He so needed to stay away from her. If she was waiting for love, he couldn't be the one to give it to her. He didn't even know what the word meant, not really.

A tuxedoed waiter passed with a silver tray and offered a canapé. Cruse took one and popped it in his mouth as he strolled to the edge of the marble balcony, leaning a hip on the edge where he could keep an eye on Bayley. He guessed this party was a fitting reminder that he and Bayley were too different to make things work between them, even if he hadn't had other obligations.

He let his eyes follow her as she mingled. What he wanted to do was glue himself to her side, her own personal body armor. If he let it, this thing with Bayley could totally distract him from the S.O.S. case. He flicked a glance to the side.

Bayley had pointed out the guest of most interest to him. Charles Hutton Stanfield III, who was currently enjoying a cigar and the attentions of a woman who was not Mrs. Charles Hutton Stanfield III. Cruse waited as Stanfield sent the little redhead on her way before walking the length of the portico to meet him.

"Mr. Stanfield, may I have a word with you?"

The older man started to decline, but as Cruse flashed his badge, gestured behind him to French doors. "I don't think Edgar will mind us using his office for a private chat."

Edgar being Edgar Foster, Bayley's dad. He'd forgotten the two men were close friends as well as neighbors. "You know the Fosters well."

Stanfield rested his cigar on a crystal ashtray and sat down behind Edgar Foster's desk. "I do. Edgar and I went to college together back East and settled here in Pensacola thirty years ago. Been friends and business partners ever since."

"I thought Mr. Foster was an attorney." Not a suspect. One more for the list. Could Bayley's father have anything to do with the S.O.S. murders? He had the reputation in court of a ruthless man. That didn't mean he'd resort to murder, but it did mean that Cruse needed to find out as much about Mr. Foster's finances as possible. See if he could take a sizable hit and stay afloat.

"Yes, with large investment holdings, like most people of wealth. Is there something I can do for you?"

Cruse sat in one of the leather chairs facing the desk.

"I'd like to talk to you about a development project called La Plage. Your company is behind the development."

"Yes, my son Thomas is the project manager. What's the problem?"

Cruse noted the signs as Stanfield grew almost imperceptibly more stressed. The fabric of his finely cut tuxedo shifted just a bit over his shoulders and his jaw tensed slightly. "Two members of a group called Save Our Shores have been murdered. This group has a history of making progress on construction projects very difficult for development companies."

"I'm aware of that. What's the point?" Stanfield picked a Montblanc pen up from the desk and began to pass it between his fingers.

"In addition, a scientist, well-known for his work in environmental studies, has been savagely beaten and is in the hospital unable to testify in a court hearing against your development."

"If you want to accuse me of something, say it like a man, Conyers," Stanfield barked.

"Sir, I just want your input. Insight into the murders or, if you don't have any, an idea of someone who might." Losing his temper with Stanfield wouldn't help anything, and it certainly wouldn't get him the answers he needed.

"I don't oversee day-to-day decisions of individual projects. With holdings around the country and overseas, I simply don't have time." The lines in Stanfield's face deepened. "Thomas is in that position for the project you've mentioned. However, he's been in Europe most of the past two months."

"Who stands to lose if La Plage cannot be completed?"

Stanfield stood abruptly and walked to the wet bar at the other end of the room, selected a crystal tumbler and poured a finger of bourbon. "Please. The cost would be too high to count. Many of the investors could lose millions, if not more. That's the nature of speculative real estate."

He tossed back the entire tumbler of liquor, breathed fire for a moment and then cleared his throat. "I will tell you that this is Thomas's last project with the company if that problem can't be worked out with the Save Our Shores group. The board of directors has exhausted their considerable patience, waiting for him to grow up."

Cruse walked over to the bar, picked up a picture of Thomas and Bayley, arm in arm. Jealousy, irrational and unwanted, stabbed through him. Just as quickly, an image of Bayley in the lifeguard stand last night came to mind and he settled.

Stanfield poured another drink, his shoulders seeming to droop just a little. "All I've ever wanted for Thomas was for him to be successful and prosperous. I've bailed him out time and time again. Maybe wanting that was a mistake. I don't know."

The doors flew open, and Bayley's father strode into the room. "What in the world is going on here?"

Cruse held his hands out—no harm. "I'm just asking Mr. Stanfield a few questions."

"As his attorney, I'm advising him to shut his mouth right now." Edgar Foster shot a disgusted look at Stanfield and went to the bar to pour himself a tumbler of whiskey.

"Take it easy, Edgar." Stanfield raised an eyebrow at Cruse. "Surely I'm not the only company who might have reason to kill one of those environmentalists?"

"No, sir, you're not. All the same, I'd like to see a list of your investors."

Foster interrupted. "I assume you don't have a warrant or we wouldn't be having this conversation."

"No, sir, I don't. Yet. But I'd appreciate some cooperation." He handed a card to Stanfield. "You can fax that list to my office. And if you think of anything else we should know I'd be grateful if you'd share it."

"Don't hold your breath, Conyers," Edgar Foster said.

A throat clearing caught their attention. Bayley stood in the door, a very annoyed expression on her face. "Gentlemen, I believe the party is outside."

Stanfield immediately disappeared out the French doors, patting his pockets, presumably for another cigar. Foster, a braver man than Cruse, stared his daughter down. "I'd like to have a word with you first, Bayley."

She turned beseeching eyes to Cruse. He'd gladly help, but did she want him to go or stay?

Foster, not playing nice like his daughter, pointed a look of his own. "Detective Conyers, please excuse us."

Crossing behind Foster, Cruse shrugged a "sorry" at Bayley and held her eyes as he backed out the doors onto the portico, closing them in front of him.

"What is it, Daddy?"

Her distinguishedly graying father, elegant in his tuxedo, poured himself a whiskey, not his first if his exaggerated care was any sign. "I wanted to make sure you're taking care of yourself. I called your office this morning and they told me you'd taken a few days off."

"I have, but obviously I'm still working. I'm here, aren't I?"

"I saw you with that detective, Bayley. He had his hands on you."

Oh, so now they were getting to the crux of the matter. "You had to know that I would date at some time in my life."

"Conyers is not right for you." He gestured out the window with his cut-crystal tumbler. "There are at least twenty single men at this party who would be better for you than him. Men with breeding and character."

"Men with money, you mean." When he shrugged, she laughed. "Now you're being ridiculous. Cruse is a good man. He likes me for who I am. Not because I have money, or because he's trying to make a good impression on you for some reason, like most of the attorneys that are here tonight."

"I don't want you seeing him anymore."

"You can't stop me, Daddy." She walked to the doors and

looked out at the benefit she'd organized. Why was he so willing to let her have a job, but he'd be hanged if he'd let her have a life? He was too used to his wife, who unfailingly gave him his way.

She knew that she and Cruse weren't dating, but things were too complicated between them to call it simple friendship. Not anymore.

Her father crossed to his desk and opened a drawer, sliding out a sheet of paper. "I wasn't going to tell you this, Bayley. But Cruse Conyers isn't what he seems."

"I know all about him. He's told me everything about his past. I'm not going to let a person's background affect my opinion of him today."

"He's told you everything."

"Yes!"

"Did he tell you I'm paying him to protect you?"

Shock held Bayley speechless. For a moment. "That's not true. I don't believe you."

He handed her the sheet of paper he held. It was a photocopy of a canceled check, made out to Cruse Conyers for twenty-five thousand dollars. She stared at the paper. "You think I'm such a loser you have to buy a man for me?"

"I bought a protector for you, Bayley. You wouldn't let me hire private security when you moved out, so I hired Conyers."

Could all of Cruse's actions, from the time she'd first seen him, have been a lie? She didn't think she could have been that wrong about him. She knew him. But if she was wrong, he'd been taking advantage of her from the start. For her father's money.

Slowly, she straightened her shoulders. "Well, Cruse may be a jerk for taking your money. But what does that make you for offering it to him? You make me ashamed to be your daughter." She walked out, scraping up every shred of dignity she possibly could to make it out the door without crying.

Outside, she found her assistant, Stacy, who gave her a quick hug. "Bayley, it's a huge success. We've had so many donations. People are going berserk to give. How did you do it?"

"I'm just a persuasive gal, I guess."

Stacy turned quick perceptive eyes on Bayley. "What's wrong?"

"I have a migraine. I need to escape before I'm sick."

Stacy nodded. "Of course, sweetie. I can handle things from here on out."

Bayley stumbled out the gate to the driveway, where she and Cruse had parked long before the valets had arrived to begin parking the guests. His battered red Jeep sat underneath the trees, and, yes—the keys were in the ignition. She slid into the seat and pulled off her heels, closing her eyes as she stretched her achy feet. A very real headache throbbed over her left eye, nausea swamping her.

Where could she go? Not back to Cruse's, and she didn't have a home to go to, not anymore. She'd have to go to a hotel. She lowered her head to the steering wheel and cranked the throaty engine.

God, how could You let this happen?

I trusted him.

She raised her head and wheeled out of the driveway, wishing she could wheel right out of Detective Cruse Conyers's life.

ELEVEN

Cruse scanned the party crowd. Where was Bayley? He'd left her with her father in his office, but Edgar Foster now mingled in a group of similarly suited men by the pier. Checking with each plainclothes cop was a no-brainer. He'd done that. No one had seen her. He'd gone through the upstairs of Bayley's childhood home himself.

In the kitchen he found Bayley's assistant, Stacy, frantically arguing with the caterer about packing up the food an hour earlier than agreed. "You can't leave or you won't work another fund-raising event for Hope House again."

"I can't work in this environment."

"*What* environment?"

He stepped between her and the caterer. "Stacy, where's Bayley?"

"Obviously not here when I need her. This woman barely speaks English."

The caterer slammed a tray of crystal glasses onto a cart and started rolling it toward the door. Cruse stepped in front of the door and pulled his coat back, showing his gun and badge. The caterer threw up her hands and stormed into the dining room.

"Thanks a lot." Stacy crossed her arms and stared at Cruse. "Do I know you?"

"I need to find Bayley. Where is she?"

"She left at least a half hour ago."

"By herself?"

"Yes, by herself. Now if you'll excuse me, I need to find someone who speaks Latvian." Stacy turned on her heel and left by the door to the dining room.

Cruse strode out the back door to the gardens. He'd dialed dispatch on his cell phone to request backup to help him hunt for Bayley, but then he stopped to think. He closed the phone slowly. If he called it in, every cop car and every scanner in the metro area would hear it. Slayton would hear it. *Everyone,* even people who didn't need to have that information, would know she was on her own.

He'd look for her himself. Sprinting for the driveway, he dialed her cell phone. "Come on, Bayley, pick up."

Foreboding sank deep into his belly. This couldn't be good.

He skidded to a stop. His Jeep was gone. Again. He felt his pockets. Empty. The pockets on the pants of this ridiculous tux had been so small, he'd left the keys in the ignition when they'd arrived—before the valets—for Bayley to set up. Smart, Bayley, remembering that.

His admiration tempered with worry and just a little irritation that she would leave without telling him. Something set her off. Something like Edgar Foster.

He opened his phone again, punching a number that unfortunately he knew by heart. "Maria? I need a ride."

A few minutes later, Fuentes pulled in, gave him the once-over. "Nice duds, Detective."

"Yay me. Scoot over."

"No way. I drive my vehicle."

Cruse sighed and folded his long legs into the passenger's side of Fuentes's SBPD-issue Crown Vic. "We're looking for Bayley driving my Jeep. Let's try my place first. If she were scared, that might be where she'll feel safe."

The way things were between them, *he* didn't feel safe there. He didn't think she did either. Unsteady, unstable, uncertain, maybe all those words applied, but *safe?* No.

"Why'd she leave the party?" Fuentes shook her head, curly brown hair swinging like a disapproving schoolmarm's finger.

"I'm guessing something spooked her, but I don't know."

"Hey, Detective." Usually Fuentes said his rank like a bad word. This time, her voice was soft, indicative. He followed her gaze as she slowed the car. His Jeep sat under a tree in the parking lot of Beachside Inn, in the shadows, but not hidden.

He drew a breath, his hand already on the door handle. "Pull in. I'll get her."

"Cruse." Maria put the car in Park and laid a gentle hand on his arm. "Why don't you let me talk to Bayley?"

He stopped halfway out, looked back at Maria. "Fine."

For ten minutes, he cooled his heels, waiting for Fuentes. In the end, she came out alone. No Bayley.

Maria slid into the car. "She's not coming out."

He started the motion to get out of the car.

"And she doesn't want to see you." The CSU tech laughed. "Man, if you feel as miserable as you look, I'm glad I'm not you. Bayley did it right, Cruse. She didn't pay with a credit card, she didn't leave ID or a name at the desk."

"And yet you were able to find her room number that easily."

Maria went silent for five full seconds. "Yeah, I was."

"I'm staying."

"No, Cruse, I'll stay. If you press her now, you'll ruin anything you might have with her. And don't say you don't care when it's so obvious that you do."

Cruse let out a short mirthless laugh. "Maria, you know there's no happy ending for cops like us."

She sighed. "Yeah, Conyers, I know, but take the night off. Okay?"

Torture had a new meaning for Cruse. Being near Bayley and not being able to get to her. Knowing that even though he wanted her more than he wanted his next breath, he had to keep his distance. Even so, he needed to talk to her, figure out what had changed, what sent her running.

And protect her however he could, whether that meant from him, or from the man determined to stalk and harm her.

The police cruiser pulled into the gated driveway at Hope House, gravel in the driveway grinding under the wheels. Bayley didn't move, but continued staring out the window at the trees blocking the windows.

Maria touched her hand. "Why don't you let your assistant handle this?"

"I need to be here. I always have a cup of tea with new clients before they settle in." She opened the door. "It'll be fine, Maria."

Walking up the back steps to the remodeled Victorian, Maria stopped her. "I have to ask—why didn't you stay here, instead of a hotel? The location is a closely held secret, the security excellent. It seems like it would be a much safer choice than a hotel, even if technically no one knew where you were."

"It probably would be safer for me. But it wouldn't be safer for them." She motioned to the scattered children playing in the backyard. The high fence notwithstanding, the backyard at Hope House was a tiny haven of normalcy.

Maria's fierce face melted into a mask of compassion.

"Oh, stop that." Bayley managed a laugh. "That face is not allowed."

Her office right outside the back door was one of her favorite places. Here in the sanctuary of her office, in the comfy chairs and safety of the quiet room, she saw the first loosening of the bonds of abuse that held her clients. Here that she felt them glean that first bit of trust. Over a simple cup of shared tea, she often became the first person to tend to them, to really listen to them in years. And she loved it.

She pushed the door open to her office and gasped. Every available surface, every square inch of her walls had been covered with eight-by-ten photographs. Pictures of her at work, at Sip This, with Sailor, and Scruffy. Cruse appeared in about half of the photos, at least the ones she could see. Her stomach pitched. There were pictures of her here. Pictures of the children—he had been here, and more than once, to take pictures of the children.

Bayley closed the door. Taking deep short breaths, she leaned against the wall in the hall, forced back the scream that welled up. Frustration, not panic.

She couldn't think about what this meant, not now. Now she had to think about her clients, the residents here, the children. *Their* safety came before her comfort zone. "Maria?"

"Yeah." Maria popped her head into the hall from the kitchen. One look at Bayley's face must have been enough because her eyes widened and she crossed to Bayley immediately. "What's going on?"

Bayley lowered her voice to a near whisper. "The stalker has been here. In my office. I need you to handle—" she waved a hand at the door "—*that* while I get the residents here moved somewhere else. We have protocols in place for a breach of security, but I need to get it rolling."

Maria nodded, her corkscrew curls bobbing. "You got it."

Ten minutes later, Bayley had the residents in the backyard, handing out keys to condos in a gated facility with twenty-four-hour security. It was a stopgap measure, but a good one. They would use vans to move the fourteen residents—women and children—to the new place.

Cruse pulled into the driveway. When Bayley swallowed hard, she realized the lump in her throat had never quite left, just been overwhelmed with more pressing emotions.

She passed the packets of keys to her assistant, Stacy. "Be right back." Bayley crossed to him, the hurt from last night still fresh and new. "What are you doing here, Cruse?"

"I heard it on the scanner." He looked at his feet, where a toy dump truck lay on its side in the sand, then back at her. "Would you expect me not to be here, Bayley?"

"No, I guess, in light of things, this is exactly where I'd expect you to be." Disappointment and anger bubbled inside her, warring for first place in her emotions.

"What does that mean?"

"Nothing, Cruse." A little boy, around four years old, circled around them, giving Cruse a wide berth. As a man, Cruse'd be suspect simply because of his gender.

Cruse picked up the toy truck and walked ten feet or so to the porch and placed it gently on one of the steps before walking back to her. "Come on, Bayley, if you have something to say, just spit it out."

The words of accusation were on the tip of her tongue, but she couldn't force herself to say them. He wasn't a bad guy. She'd just seen him move a toy so an abused child didn't have to be afraid of his size. "I can't talk about it right now."

"Fine." He turned and walked away.

Bayley shook her head and returned to the small group of residents of Hope House as the vans pulled into the driveway. Disbelief sat like a rock in her gut, that the stalker had been able to reach her even here. "These vans will take you to the new location and Stacy will help you get settled. I'll be there to check on you later today. If you need anything, let us know. Don't be afraid. We're taking care of the situation."

Angel, the mom with the two tiny children, stopped Bayley with a soft hand on her arm. "Who's taking care of you?"

Bayley's heart squeezed. "I'll be fine." Her gaze found Cruse, talking with the CSU techs on the other side of the yard, waiting at a respectful distance until the residents left.

As the vans drove away, Bayley climbed the stairs into the kitchen, stopping to drop into a kitchen chair and catch her breath. She glanced out the window that the CSU tech had opened to dust and heard Cruse say from the back porch, "Hey, man."

Slayton advanced on Cruse, an avenging angel look on his darkly tanned face. "Time to tell me what's going on, Cruse."

"I don't know what you mean."

"Yes, you do." Slay was flaming mad, no doubt about that. "You messed up true this time and called this in through dispatch. I heard it go out over the radio. And when I asked, guess what I found out? This is the third time this week CSU's been called for Bayley."

Cruse stayed in his relaxed position. "That's right."

Slayton's black eyes burned with hurt hostility. "Are you so jealous of her that you're deliberately keeping me out of this case? Because that's just stupid."

"I'm not shutting you out because I'm jealous," Cruse said, taking care to keep his voice even and quiet. "I'm shutting you out because you're a suspect."

Shock blanked the hurt out of Slay's face.

How could Cruse do this? The Cruse she thought she knew would never take money from her father or accuse his partner of being a stalker. Hurt mingled with curiosity as Bayley stopped trying to pretend she wasn't listening and leaned closer to the window.

"You went to college with Bayley. You were right there when it all started, Slay. And you didn't say a word. Now let's talk about who's keeping secrets."

The anger bled out of Slay's body and he slumped into a sitting position on an iron chair behind him. Cruse sat down opposite him, a small decorative table between them.

Slayton went to her college? Maybe *she* would finally get some answers, too. After all the questions, all the protecting, it had to be time.

"Cruse, I didn't tell you about college because I honestly didn't think it was important. It was a big campus!"

Cruse shook his head before Slay even finished talking. "Try again. I'm not buying that. You and I both know that a witness from the time of the initial incident is valuable. You might have remembered something that could crack this case wide-open."

Slay rubbed the heels of his hand over his eyes. "Okay, the real truth is, I was embarrassed. I was a scrawny kid who worked in the school cafeteria. And, yeah, I knew Bayley. Everybody on campus did. She was gorgeous, rich and smart. As far as I know, I never even spoke to her. She wouldn't have remembered."

Cruse sighed. "Slayton, you're my partner. Do you think I *want* you to be a suspect? I *want* you to prove you're innocent. But what you're saying doesn't help you."

Slayton rose to his feet. "Cruse, you're talking crazy. I'm not a stalker, and I shouldn't be a suspect."

"What about the flowers?" Cruse stood and joined Slay at the porch rail. She eased to the screened door where she could hear better, her stomach churning as detail after detail of what Cruse had been keeping from her came out.

Slayton's eyebrows slammed together in a picture of confusion, his fingers tapping a crazy drumbeat on the rail. "What flowers?"

"The roses? You bought two dozen red roses from Gloria. One went to your mother but the other you kept to deliver yourself."

"I can't believe you're actually accusing me. I took the other roses because I'm involved with someone. I took them myself because I didn't want 'Gloria the Gossip Mill' to know who they were for."

"Who were they for?"

"You're really going to make me do this?"

"Who were they for?"

"Cora." Slayton whispered it, looking around the porch behind him to make sure they weren't overheard. Bayley stepped away from the screened door so he wouldn't see her, but went quickly back when he looked at Cruse again.

"Officer Massey? Cora Massey?" Cruse's voice was incredulous.

"Cruse, quiet down. I could get Cora in trouble if that got out."

Cruse's eyes bored into Slayton's. He looked nothing like the man she knew, and everything like the cold cop she didn't want to know. "I'm going to have to ask her about it."

Slayton stepped away from Cruse, eyes narrowing in a look of near hatred. "You do what you have to do, Cruse. Then you can start looking for another partner. I'm not going to be teamed up with someone who doesn't trust me." He snapped a turn and walked down the stairs off the porch, not looking back.

Cruse stared out at the playground equipment, an empty swing twisting in the breeze. Bayley stood at the back door, fixed in disbelief. How could he keep something that huge from her? This wasn't classified information. It wasn't even the fact that he was taking money to be with her. This was her life. *Hers.*

Cruse started back toward the door, looking up to see her face. When he caught sight of her, he stopped in the middle of the deck and his shoulders dropped. "You heard?"

She nodded, unsaid accusations—the canceled check, his keeping secrets—like shards of glass in her throat.

"Do you want to talk about it?" Cruse almost looked like he wanted her to say no, but she couldn't let this slide. She was sick to death of being protected. People who claimed to care were always trying to shield her from life. And the same thing happened—she got shut out.

A knot of disappointment—in Cruse, and in herself for believing in him—lay like lead in Bayley's stomach. She'd given him chance after chance. Was it time to face the fact that he'd been too burned by what he'd experienced with his sister, by his cop mentality, to ever be able to let go of the control?

She'd started to believe that maybe he could be her soul mate, the person that God had sent to be hers—her best friend for the rest of her life. How could she have been so wrong?

"I don't know what to say, Cruse. I can't believe that you didn't tell me about Slay. I'm so incredibly sick of being sheltered from things that affect *me*."

Cruse stood unmoving while she snapped. She'd grown accustomed to his unnatural stillness, but this was different. Maybe it was emotion that held him in place, or maybe it was just bone-deep weariness.

"You don't get it, Bayley. I wasn't trying to protect you. I was trying to protect *Slayton*."

"What?"

His voice dropped to an intent whisper. "I had to conclusively prove that he wasn't your stalker. If even a whisper of that kind of suspicion got out, his career could have been over." His voice rose a hair. "And you need to realize that you've been allowed far more access to information in this case than protocol allows. I've put myself and my career on the line every single day because I was scared to let you out of my sight."

Bayley took a step back. How did he do that? Every time she wanted to yell at him, he managed to say the one thing that could make her want to hold on to him instead. But there was one thing he hadn't mentioned, one thing that couldn't be explained away.

"Cruse, what about this?" She pulled the square of folded paper out of her back pocket and slapped it into his hands.

Cruse unfolded the paper, smoothing it carefully. He didn't say a word, just laid it down on the table. The ocean-green eyes that she loved met hers and the hurt in them nearly bowled her over. Still he didn't speak.

His cell phone rang and he didn't answer it, just silenced it without looking at it. "I didn't take the money, Bayley. Your father wouldn't take no for an answer, so I cashed the check and donated the money to Hope House. Believe it or not, I don't need your father's money. I have plenty of my own."

The twenty-five-thousand-dollar anonymous donor. Bayley stood there and stared at Cruse. She was as bad as her father, making assumptions. The shame that swamped her could have been avoided if she'd had faith.

Instead, she'd let it all be about her. *Her* insecurities and *her* need for independence overrode everything else, even to the point that she closed her eyes to what was right there in front of her.

Cruse's cell phone chirped at him. With an impatient shrug, he snatched it off his waist and checked a text message. Giving her one last tired look, he walked to the other side of the porch to return the call.

Bayley stood rooted to the spot, her mind running unerringly to the only conclusion that made sense. Cruse protected the ones he cared about. He loved Slay, and Sailor, and at least cared about her. None of them had understood that, with the possible exception of Sailor. Bayley pushed him away because he was protective, robbing him of his best way of showing that he cared.

Bayley, even though she was so concerned that money didn't represent who she was, didn't take a minute to be sure that she saw the reason for Cruse's protectiveness and not just what she wanted to see. And she had thought only about her need for freedom when she should have realized that Cruse...Cruse kept her safe. In so many more ways than the physical.

He ended his call and let out a piercing whistle. Within seconds, a cop she recognized came bounding around the corner of the house. His respect for Cruse was evident. A small smile tugged at the corner of Bayley's mouth.

Cruse *was* a person to respect. A person to lean on and trust. Maybe even to love.

"Bayley, come here, please." When Bayley stood beside him, he said evenly, "This is Officer Joe Sheehan. He's going to stay here with you."

"Wait, Cruse, I—"

"I don't have time to talk, Bayley."

She nodded and Cruse left without a backward glance, leaving Bayley's unfinished sentence hanging in the air. Silently, she finished it. *I need to say I'm sorry.*

Cruse lifted the crime-scene tape and bent to dip underneath it. Cops swarmed the scene, parting to let Cruse pass. This murder had been connected to the S.O.S. case, the theory being that Judge Schilling had been killed because he was slated to begin the process of injunction for the La Plage property. Schilling had a reputation for being sympathetic to the environmentalists. Rumor had it he'd even given money under the table to S.O.S.

Cruse found the officer in charge. "Hey, Cora. What've you got?"

All business, Cora Massey fired off the facts. "He was killed getting into his car to go home. Once shots were fired, security caught the perp on video surveillance. He'd set up on the roof of the parking deck directly to the south."

"Wait. You got the guy on video? Any ID yet?"

"You didn't hear? We caught the guy leaving the deck. Wonders never cease, security actually mobilized quick enough to catch the guy. He's in holding over at county."

"Cora, you deserve a medal." Finally, the lead he'd been waiting for.

"Hold on, cowboy. There's no way this guy is the mastermind behind the S.O.S. murders. He's brute strength only." Cora glanced to the side as one of the other officers called her name. "Gotta run."

Slayton walked up beside Cruse, just missing Cora, who didn't glance back. She was either studiously ignoring Slay to keep up the pretense or he'd been lying about their relationship, too. Cruse definitely needed to have a conversation with Cora when things weren't so hectic.

Slay listened, arms folded across his chest, as Cruse quickly filled him in. "I think it's time to get a search warrant for Thomas Stanfield's beach house. He's the only viable suspect."

Cruse nodded. "Go ahead and make the call. I don't think we'll have any trouble with the judge, considering one of their own just got gunned down."

Slay started to walk away.

"Slayton," Cruse called.

His partner turned and looked back at him, his dark features shuttered.

Cruse walked to meet him. "I'm sorry. I didn't know any other way to protect you."

"I don't know how you could suspect me of doing those things to Bayley, Cruse."

"I know."

Slayton just shook his head and walked away, pulling out

his cell phone, leaving Cruse free to second-guess himself. He knew Slay, so how could he have suspected him? But as a cop, with the facts he had, how could he not?

He'd tried to protect his partner. Still, despite his best efforts, he'd failed yet another person he cared about. How could this happen? He did his best to do what God asked of him, to pray for guidance, to follow what he knew was right. And still people he cared about ended up hurt.

Where was the justice in that?

He took a deep breath and remembered that God had not promised a perfect walk, perfect solutions. Sometimes life was just life. And because God had given them the right to make their own choices, it was not always ideal. *Keep secrets, not keep secrets, choose Him, not choose Him, walk away, stick around and see things through.* Sometimes sticking around was the hardest thing to do.

He called Sailor, secured her promise to be on the watch for Bayley when she left Hope House, and ducked back under the bright-yellow crime-scene boundary. With any luck, Slayton would have that warrant within the hour and he'd be inside Stanfield's base here in town.

Regret reared up in Cruse—not for taking aim at a murderer, but that in doing so, he'd be hurting Bayley. No compromising this though: if Thomas Stanfield ordered those murders, he was a monster who deserved to go down.

Cruse's cell phone chirped. He checked the text readout. Time to roll. He jumped into his Jeep and turned it back to the beach house. Adrenaline coursed through his body, making his fingertips tingle.

His focus narrowed to a single intense point. *Take down a killer.*

Every piece of evidence lined up perfectly.

The e-mails, found on Thomas Stanfield's computer, nailed him: "After key S.O.S. operatives have been eliminated, this project can move forward with no further obstacles to progress." Before Bayley found the body: "Time to take action against S.O.S., starting with the leadership—Frank Watson, followed by Brad Paxton." And after Frederick Hughes's murder: "Excellent job. Payment deposited in Cayman account."

Cruse glanced at the dashboard clock. 1:00 a.m. He turned his blinker on as he eased around the corner on his street.

The interrogation of the hit man was ongoing, but Cruse had heard enough to convince him that he'd been hired by Thomas Stanfield. The man had held out for a while, but when it became clear to him that keeping quiet was detrimental to his future health, he didn't hesitate to implicate Thomas.

Most incriminating, and shocking, had been the materials they found in Thomas's beach house.

Within a matter of hours, they had closed the case and Thomas had been hauled away to jail with a surprising lack of resistance or objection. It should have been satisfying. But Cruse had never felt more empty about putting a criminal away.

What madness caused a man to step away from right and go so wrong? A man who had every luxury given him?

In Cruse's mind, Thomas Stanfield only proved that no man could live without God. That no amount of money could make up for a lack of love.

After twenty-one hours on his feet, his dark, quiet house was a welcome relief. He'd gotten the message that Sailor and Bayley had gone to his house, but they must have gone to bed, a relief in its own way.

Cruse shuffled into the kitchen, opened the refrigerator door and leaned on it because he was too tired to stand up straight.

"If you're interested, I left you a sandwich on the second shelf." Sailor's disembodied voice came from the direction of the sofa.

"So you are awake." Cruse took the plate out with the ham

sandwich, and grabbed a bag of cheddar-and-sour-cream potato chips off the counter. He kicked the door shut with the back of his foot.

Sailor turned one of the end-table lights on as Cruse settled on the couch beside her. "I was sleeping, but I wanted to talk to you when you got home."

He spoke around a mouthful of ham sandwich. "Is Bayley okay?"

"She's worried about you." Sailor dug in Cruse's potato chip bag and pulled out a handful of chips.

"Hey, get out of my chips." Cruse moved the bag to the other side of him and got a chuckle out of Sailor. "The cases are closed now. She can stop worrying."

"I don't think that's what she's worrying about, Cruse." She rolled her eyes. "I swear men are so clueless."

"Sailor, I'm being patient with you because you made me a sandwich, but I'm tired and I don't want to talk about this right now."

"What's she going to be to you when it's not your job to protect her anymore?"

Clearly, his sister didn't know the meaning of "I don't want to talk about this right now." Cruse sighed and put down the remains of his sandwich. "She's not going to be anything to me, Sailor. She's going to go back to her nice life and I'm going to go back, hopefully, to surfing more and being a cop less."

"How can you say that? She's the best thing that's ever happened to you."

"Maybe so, but I'm not the best thing that ever happened to her. Can you honestly see someone like her with someone like me?"

"Yes! I don't know where you got your inferiority complex, but you need to take a look in the mirror."

Exhaustion kept him from guarding his words. "I look in

the mirror every day and see the man that failed you when you needed me most, Sailor."

When he looked back at Sailor, she was on her feet, hands on hips, and he would have sworn fire shot out of her eyes. "Cruse Conyers. You need to get this straight right now. You did *not* fail me. You were a kid. And the only regret I have is that we didn't leave that stinking rathole earlier."

She sat down in front of Cruse on the coffee table and took his face in her hands like he was still a little boy. "Honey, listen to me. One person is no more worthy of love than another. Push comes to shove, we're all unworthy. If you know what's good for you, you won't walk away."

Cruse, muscles rebelling with a bone-deep ache, had no more energy for argument. "I'll think about it, Sailor."

"Well, while you're thinking, think on this. God doesn't expect perfection and Bayley doesn't need *your idea* of perfect, either. She needs a flesh and blood man who loves her more than anything else in this world. Who loves her enough to put all those excuses aside and just go for it."

Sailor dropped a kiss on his head and disappeared into her bedroom, leaving Cruse alone, trying to figure out when he'd gone back to being five years old.

On the way to his own room, he hesitated as he passed the guest-room door, cracked open to the hall. He thought twice, and then eased the door open. Scruff raised his head and thumped his tail, still keeping watch over Bayley. A smile drifted across Cruse's face. A short-lived smile. Because weighing heavy on his mind was the fact that, in the morning, he had to face Bayley.

And somehow find a way to tell her that her best friend had been arrested tonight.

TWELVE

Rumpled and bed-headed, Bayley stumbled into the kitchen the next morning in search of coffee, only to pull up short when she saw Cruse already at the pot. Smart man, he took one look at her and poured another cup.

Bayley smoothed her bedraggled T-shirt over long pajama pants. She felt at a distinct disadvantage. Cruse had obviously been up for a while and had already showered and dressed for work. His faded T-shirt rode up over the gun attached to his hip.

She hadn't wanted to come back to his house, hadn't wanted to be dependent on him. Sailor had convinced her that he'd needed her to be safe, so he could do his job without distraction. And she'd needed to be close to him, so she could apologize when she had the chance.

"Bayley," he said quietly, "there are some things we need to talk about. I hate to do it right now, but I've got to get back to work."

That sounded…foreboding, almost. Bayley swallowed hard, the coffee burning as it went down. She followed him out onto the screened porch and sat in one of the padded deck chairs, the sound of the rolling surf a familiar murmur in the background.

"If this is about yesterday, Cruse, I'd like to talk about it."

He held up a hand, but she rushed to get through the rest of it. "For the past few years, I've felt so smothered. My family—they meant well—but their answer to the stalking situation was to not let me have a life. When all this started again, I felt all the independence I'd gained slip away little by little. And I forgot that being protected isn't always a bad thing. That the people who are doing the protecting are doing it because it's their job."

She held his eyes tenaciously. "Or because they care."

With one look at his face, she could tell that he wasn't going to accept her apology. "I'm sorry I didn't just ask you about the check from my dad. I knew you wouldn't take the money. I even told him that. I guess that's what makes him such a good attorney. He had you convicted with circumstantial evidence in the space of sixty seconds."

His expression, far from being unreadable, scared her. "Cruse, are you okay?"

"Forget about what happened yesterday. The way you responded when you found out about Slayton was perfectly understandable. And the money thing—I should have just told you straight out. I don't know why I didn't." He hesitated. "I'm not used to including other people in my life."

"O-*kay*." She should be relieved, but Cruse didn't look right. If anything, the grooves in his face seemed deeper. Bayley's heart started to pound. "What's wrong?"

"There's no easy way to say this, so I'm going to just say it. Last night, a federal judge was shot and killed by the S.O.S. killer." Bayley gasped, but Cruse didn't stop. "Because Thomas was our best suspect, we were able to get a search warrant for the beach house. I promise, Bayley, as much as I wanted to solve this case, I didn't want Thomas to be guilty."

Panic started to creep up on Bayley. "He's *not* guilty."

Cruse's steady voice soothed her raw edges even as the words he said wounded her. "In the home office, we found enough evidence to put Thomas away for a long time. We've still got to process a lot of things, but the e-mails in his computer alone are probably enough."

Bayley shook her head, wanting to run away like a child with her hands over her ears. *La, la, la. I'm not listening to you.* "I don't believe it. I don't believe Thomas would do those things."

"He didn't do the killings himself. He ordered someone else to do them."

"No!" She stepped back, her hands raised defensively. "That's not the Thomas I know."

"That's just it, Bayley. He wasn't acting like the Thomas you know. There's no way of knowing what desperation drove him to act that way." He reached for her hands but she pulled away.

"No."

"Bayley, please sit down. There's more."

She walked to the edge of the porch, staring at the ocean, as if it held an answer to the turmoil she felt. Instead, the memory of being nearly swept to sea by the rip current overwhelmed her. "Just tell me."

"We found copies of the pictures. The ones pasted all over your office at Hope House."

"Cruse, what are you saying?"

"Thomas was your stalker."

Bayley didn't recognize the keening sound she heard as coming from her. As far as she could tell, it was caught up in the black storm of images that whirled at her from every direction. She and Thomas in their tree house, as each other's prom date, dead birds, dead body, slashed tires, *fear.* Always the fear.

She felt herself being shoved into a chair and her head being pushed between her knees. "Come on, honey. Breathe."

After a moment, the dizziness subsided, and Bayley could

sit up. One look at Cruse's concerned face, though, and she lost it again. Huge, wrenching sobs broke free from her chest. As he pulled her into his arms—big, strong and safe—and they closed protectively around her, she prayed that in all the wrong, perhaps, just this one thing could be right.

"Bayley, you don't have to do this." Cruse held a death grip on her elbow, steering her down the hall at the police station, as if she was going to keel over if he didn't keep hold of her.

"I do have to. I have to see Thomas for myself." It would be one of the hardest things she'd ever have to do. Fragile from this morning's emotional outburst, she'd have to dig deep to find the strength. She had to believe that Thomas would do the same for her.

"You'll maybe have ten minutes. I couldn't get you any more time than that. His arraignment is this morning at eleven. And I'm sorry, but I have to stay in the interview room with you."

"Cruse, you told me. It's fine." His expression, somewhere between worried and nauseated, made her smile. "Seriously, I'll be okay. I've had my breakdown."

Cruse stopped at a gunmetal-gray steel door. "He's been in holding, but they brought him to an interview room. He'll be handcuffed to the table and his feet will be shackled."

Bayley took a deep breath. "I'm ready."

But she wasn't. She was totally unprepared for the sight of her lifelong friend chained to the table like a common criminal. The smell of sweat stung her eyes, the odor of evil and fear hanging heavy in the air, from so many that had sat in that chair before Thomas.

When he raised his eyes, Bayley was stunned. No hint of defiance showed in his countenance, only the bleak evidence of a defeated man. His hollow expression didn't change when he saw her, but his pale-blue eyes filled.

She hurried to the table and sat across from him, reaching both hands across the scarred surface. Out of the corner of her eye, she saw Cruse lean back against the door, but he stayed out of their way.

"Bayley, why are you here?" Thomas's voice, weak and thready, made her already battered heart ache.

"I want you to tell me you didn't do this."

"I can't tell you that." He also couldn't meet her eyes.

"Thomas, why?"

He shook his head.

"Talk to me," she demanded. "If you expect me to believe that you killed people and made my life a living nightmare, you'd better talk to me. I'm not kidding, Thomas Stanfield."

For a moment, she thought he didn't hear her. His despair hovered, a living thing in the room. "I should have died instead of Charlie. I've been a disappointment to my father from day one. Don't bother arguing, you know it better than anybody."

"I don't understand."

"I couldn't disappoint him again. I'll do whatever it takes."

Bayley didn't think her heart could break any more, but seeing Thomas like this and knowing what he'd done, to her and to others, almost doubled her over with the physical pain. "What does that have to do with me? Why torment me? I don't understand."

Hazy confusion drew his eyes to hers. "What?"

"The stalking! Thomas, why?"

He stared at her unblinking for a few long seconds and his eyes filled again. A ghost of a smile whispered across his face before he said, "Everybody always said we'd make the perfect couple."

"That's no answer! Thomas, talk to me."

His voice dropped to an anguished whisper. "I can't."

For a moment, she stared at the man she'd called friend from the time she'd taken her first step. He'd stolen her life as she knew it, and ordered the deaths of four people. She couldn't fathom it.

Cruse touched her shoulder. "Bayley, it's time to go."

Without another word, she stood and walked out the door.

Slayton waited in the hall for them, concern for Bayley on his face. Cruse knew—now that they had the evidence against Thomas Stanfield—how wrong he had been to suspect his partner and his friend. But was Bayley's unswerving faith in Thomas any better? She'd been blindsided by his guilt, and torn apart.

Slayton stepped forward and with a look at Cruse, not really for permission, but just for understanding, maybe, he reached for Bayley and tugged her to him. She held on to Slay, her hands fisted in his shirt, as if the struggle to stand upright was almost more than she could handle. Cruse couldn't imagine how she must have felt, finding that the friend she'd depended on and loved her whole life was a monster.

It all came back to illusions. He prayed for the clarity to see the truth—about himself, as Sailor dared him to do, and others. It wouldn't be easy to challenge his long-held beliefs, but he wanted to grow. He wanted to change.

Slayton set Bayley back on her feet. "I'm sorry for your loss, kiddo." He tugged on a piece of Bayley's hair, eliciting a hint of a smile, before he stepped back to let them pass.

They took the stairs down. Cruse opened the door to the passenger's side for her. She flashed him a halfhearted smile and slid into the Jeep. "I don't really want to go to my house, but Mrs. Phillips said I could stay on her pull-out couch tonight until I can get my place cleaned up."

She chewed on the corner of her bottom lip. "Do you mind giving me a ride there?"

Something akin to hurt flared before Cruse squelched it firmly. "You're welcome to stay at my place. Sailor wouldn't mind coming back out there to stay tonight."

She shook her head. "No, you don't need to protect me anymore. I'm not going to impose on you and Sailor. I don't want to impose on anyone. Could you just take me to Mrs. P's?"

"I'll take you wherever you want to go." He'd known she would pull away from him. How could she not? He'd expected it, he'd planned for it, he'd prayed about it. Prepared as he'd been to lose her, he hadn't expected it to feel like he'd been hit by a truck.

After picking up Bayley's bag at Cruse's house, he walked her down the street to Mrs. Phillips's. The stricken expression on her face ate at him.

"Bayley, I could stay for a while." Mrs. Phillips's car wasn't in the driveway.

She turned to look at him then, her dark-blue eyes almost black from suppressed emotion.

"No, I know where the key is," she said firmly. "You go ahead and leave. I'll be fine."

Striding away, she stumbled on the bottom step and his body jerked, wanting to go after her, but she righted herself and walked on, not looking back.

Bayley closed the door of Mrs. Phillips's house and looked at her surroundings. Her guts ached with so much wrenching pain, she could be in a box and it wouldn't matter. She thought that she would be relieved when everything was over, but instead, all she felt was this huge gaping hole where she used to have hope.

She got a bottle of water out of the fridge, kicked off her shoes and opened the sliding glass door.

The vast expanse of the Gulf of Mexico stretched out in front of her. White sand edged aqua-green water and gently faded into navy blue. From her spot on the porch deck, she could hear the laughing squeals of the children as they flirted with disaster at the edge of the ocean. Some would scream and run with full-bodied abandon into the oncoming surf, emerging victorious.

She'd give just about anything to be able to face life like that, but after battling fear for so long, she didn't know if life could ever be normal again. Once she'd thought it could be. But there'd been so much loss, so much pain. Physically, she was fine, even healthy. Inside, she felt battered and worn. Lonely.

She'd sent Cruse away. He had gone above and beyond for her again and again. But, thinking on it now, had he ever really given her reason to assume he felt anything for her besides friendship and a sense of responsibility?

She needed to give him time to sort through his feelings for her now that she wasn't under his protection anymore. She couldn't keep leaning on him, not knowing if he was allowing it out of some sense of obligation to her. She couldn't keep leaning, period. He didn't deserve that, and she didn't need him.

She was on her own. And wasn't that the way she'd wanted it? She'd wanted to protect herself, to teach herself to be independent. For years all she'd wanted was autonomy. Now she had it, and all she could think about was how much she missed Cruse.

Everywhere she looked on the tourist-covered beach, she saw families flying kites, friends throwing Frisbees or simply sitting in harmony. Everyone seemed to be having fun—smiling, talking, playing. Laughter drifted up from the beach on the wind. Everybody had someone.

The empty room loomed behind her, silent and dark.

She'd sent Cruse away. And she'd never felt more alone.

Cruse stopped outside Mrs. Phillips's dark house and argued with himself. 3:00 a.m. He did not need to wake

Bayley up. She was exhausted and needed her rest. Not to mention that she hadn't wanted him. She'd wanted to be alone. The least he could do was give her that.

But he couldn't walk away.

He tapped on the door. If she didn't answer, he'd leave. "Bayley? It's Cruse."

His voice was strained. He let himself lean on the door frame to Mrs. P's front room and wait. He didn't hear anything.

But then she answered the door, wearing a hot-pink tank top and brightly colored polka-dotted pajama pants. Almost against his will, his mouth kicked up in a half smile.

"Come on in, Cruse."

He didn't move. Then shook his head. "I shouldn't have come here. You've been through enough."

Cruse still didn't move.

He didn't want to leave, and he didn't want to burden her with more pain. But after the night he'd had, he couldn't go home.

Instead of insisting, she took his hand and pulled him back outside. Still thinking of him and his preference for open space, even though she'd been through the wringer today.

Pushing him into a cushioned sunbathing chair, she sat in the other one, still with the tight grip on his hand. He leaned his head back and closed his eyes. How could it feel so right, this need for her? It went way beyond physical attraction, beyond cop and client, beyond friendship.

"Cruse, what's wrong? Did something happen?"

"There was a wreck on Highway 98." He swallowed hard. "A family. Ambulances took the parents to the hospital. They...had to life-flight one child. And the other one...the little girl, she didn't make it. I had to notify the grandmother and take her to the hospital to be with the baby. To tell her one child was fighting for her life and the other..."

He couldn't get it out. It had been so bad. And when it was over, all he could think about was getting to Bayley, how much he needed her vitality when death had been so near tonight.

"I just wanted to see you."

"I'm glad you came."

"Are you?" He lifted her fingers, fiddled with them. "How could you be? This is my life, Bayley. There's not that much good stuff. But there's a lot of bad."

"You know what? You're right." She faced him square on. "There's a lot of bad. And you carry some of that with you. But, Cruse, that's just life. There's good stuff and bad and it's absolutely wonderfully chaotic and messy. I'm glad you came."

She pressed her lips to his, her warmth and life pouring into him. His arms were closing around her when she pushed back.

His lips formed a protest, but she climbed to her feet and disappeared into Mrs. P's. When she came back, her arms were full of blankets. She tossed them on her chair and pushed it up next to his. Crawling up beside him, she put her head on his shoulder, wrapping her arm around his ribs. He let his arm drop around her shoulders and pulled her even closer, tight up against him. He grabbed one of the blankets with his free hand and settled it over the top of them.

Closing his eyes, he rested. He'd been right to find her. This—whatever it was between them—was simply right.

Bayley's eyes slammed open as the familiar aroma wound its way into her senses. Cruse stood beside her on the balcony with two cups of coffee. She squinted up at the sky. It was barely pink. "What's the matter with you? It's nighttime."

"Not hardly. I've got to get back to work this morning."

Bayley pushed herself out of the crouched position she'd fallen asleep in and reached for the cup, closing both hands around the hot brew. She sniffed. "At least you were smart enough to bring coffee before you left."

"Bagels, too. For you and Mrs. P."

"I think I love you." Her heart stumbled as she said the words, not knowing until they came out of her mouth that she meant every syllable.

Cruse laughed. "I wish I'd known when we met that it was this simple to make you happy."

Still stunned from her revelation, she forced a smile. "Don't need diamonds or pearls, but a good bagel...well, it's priceless." She sipped from her cup, gasping as the hot liquid scalded her mouth.

Cruse's characteristic stillness and lethal grace were in evidence this morning as he stood at the balcony rail looking out over the ocean. His strong profile attracted her, but not as much as the strong heart. *She loved him.* Truly. Not just bagel love, but real love. Forever. And mercy, but that stunned her still.

He turned back to her. "I've got to go. Thanks for letting me in this morning." He hesitated, seeming to have words on his lips, but if he did, he didn't say them. Just walked away.

What if he walked for good? She'd just figured it out. The thing that had been eluding her all this time. She'd been wanting her independence. She'd fought for it, scrambled to attain it, tried everything in the book to prove to herself that she had it. But in reality, it wasn't what she needed.

It wasn't independence that made life worth living; it was being dependent on one another. On the God who loved them. The point wasn't that she *had* to do it alone. The point was that she *couldn't* do it alone.

She'd been so busy pushing Cruse away that she hadn't understood he was just as heartily pushing her away. They were both trying to convince themselves that they didn't need anyone.

But it wasn't about being independent. It was about being *inter*dependent, that triangle of God and man. She'd been such a fool.

She just hoped it wasn't too late to show Cruse how very wrong she'd been, and how right they could be together.

Cruse walked to his desk in his office and gave his chair a spin. Cases closed, he searched for the familiar sense of satisfaction, of a job well done, but it remained elusive.

What a sad commentary on his life that he'd rather be here with nothing to do than in his home alone with his thoughts. But then maybe it was the thoughts he wanted to avoid. His beach house overflowed with memories of Bayley. Memories he had no business holding close.

Cruse brushed the dust off the blank surface of his desk, the only thing there a bobbling hula girl the guys had given him as a joke. Scruffy laid his head on Cruse's leg and whined. Absently, Cruse scratched him behind the ears.

"Hey, Cruse," a voice called from behind him.

When he turned, Cora Massey walked toward him, a couple of file folders in her hand.

"Hey, Cora. I thought you'd have been out of here by now. Don't you have a big date tonight, now that our cases are closed? I saw the roses on your desk."

She gave him a strange look, and then reached to ruffle the fur on Scruffy's head. "I'm on duty. Anyway, I think those roses were a joke on me. I don't even know who gave them to me. They just appeared on my desk."

Cruse's eyes snapped up to meet Cora's as she handed him the files. "These papers were faxed in a while ago, but with the excitement of the judge being killed and all, I guess they just didn't get to you."

"Thanks, Cora."

He'd asked for the arrest file of Judge Schilling's assassin, and what do you know, Stanfield had finally come through with the investor list. A little late, Cruse would say, but at least now he had something to do.

A niggling feeling of doubt that had started when Cora mentioned her flowers roared to life now, Cruse's instincts on full alert as he flipped the file open on his desk.

The assassin who killed Judge Schilling had a record a mile long. Arrests dating back ten years, and all over the south. He'd even been arrested here. A name jumped out at Cruse. Arresting officer: Slayton Cross.

A sick certainty creeping in on him, he opened the other file, the list of investors in La Plage. With bumbling, nervous fingers he flipped the page. And there it was, the one piece of evidence they'd been missing from the beginning. *The single person who had enough motive to kill.*

And if they had the wrong man in jail for the murders and the two cases were connected, that meant Bayley was still in danger.

Already halfway down the stairs, Scruff at his heels, he dialed her phone number as he went airborne over the last eight steps. He hit the parking lot and sprinted for his Jeep, praying he wouldn't be too late, that this wouldn't become the moment he had feared—that one time he couldn't keep her safe.

THIRTEEN

Bayley figured cleaning every inch of her house might help her to stay in it without memories of her space being violated. She walked into the bedroom, looking at the bed that she had just stripped, remembering the mussed covers, the creepy feeling of someone unknown being in her bed. She suppressed a shudder and turned the volume up on the TV. The better to block out unwanted thoughts. Talk-show entertainment news, something mindless to listen to while she worked.

She picked up the Lysol can, spraying until it emptied as the background noise changed from the closing music of the talk show to the early evening news. Bayley picked up the clicker. The last thing she wanted to watch was news. She put her finger on the channel button, but video began rolling of the most recent police press conference touting the closure of the S.O.S. murder case.

Cruse stood beside the chief of police, arms crossed over his chest. She stepped closer to the screen, reaching a hand out to touch Cruse's face as they zoomed in on him. She wished she knew what the future held. Cruse had walked away from her so many times. And she'd returned the favor.

She knew now that she wasn't going to do any more walking—she was ready to stand and fight. But was Cruse ready? Would Cruse ever be ready for someone like her?

The camera panned and Slayton's handsome features appeared next to Cruse. A breeze blew a piece of his hair across his face and he raised his hand to slide it back into place.

Bayley sucked a quick breath in. Her eyes snapped to the pile of jewelry on her dresser. No bracelet.

She dropped to her knees and searched the floor, knowing as she did that she wouldn't find it. Because it wasn't there. It was on Slayton's wrist. And in her panic over someone being in her house, she'd forgotten to tell Cruse about it.

She had to call Cruse right now. Muting the TV, she picked up her cell phone, quickly scrolling through the numbers to Cruse's. Her finger on the send button, she paused. They'd pinned the crimes on Thomas. How could the bracelet be on Slayton's wrist?

"Hello, Bayley."

Bayley froze, and slowly turned around to find Slayton lounging in her doorway. She pasted a smile on her face. "Slay, what are you doing here? I thought you'd be out celebrating that the case is closed."

He took a step into the room, holding a hand out as if calling her to him. "I came by to check on you."

She took an involuntary step back, her eyes glued to the bracelet on his wrist.

He sighed. "I see you recognize the bracelet. I'm really sorry about that, too. All this work with no mistakes and a faulty clasp messes the whole thing up."

"I...I don't know what you're talking about, Slayton."

"I wish I could believe you, Bayley, but there's too much at stake."

Her blood chilled as an ugly black gun with a silencer attached appeared in his hand. She bobbled the cell phone behind her back.

He kept the gun trained on her. "Killing you wasn't part

of the original plan. I had hoped that once Stanfield was put away for a nice long prison sentence, you and Cruse would be too busy making those sad puppy-love eyes at each other to notice my increased wealth. I tried to keep you busy, the two of you, but you had to keep putting your nose where it didn't belong."

The world—which had seemed blurry and unfocused since she found out Thomas was her stalker, and a killer—came into harsh clarity.

Slayton was the murderer. He had been pulling the strings all along.

"Why, Slay? Why did you kill all those people?"

He shook his head, a pitying look on his face. "Money. Why else? I sank everything I had, every bit of money my family had, into that development. When the S.O.S. idiots came along, trying to get court orders to stop progress, I couldn't let them."

So Slay killed them all. And since he knew that Thomas was on thin ice with the board of directors, he realized that her friend would be the perfect scapegoat. What she couldn't figure was why Thomas went along with it. "Thomas is innocent, but he's taking the rap for you. Why?"

"Your friend isn't as innocent as you think, Bayley. I caught him in a DUI a couple months back. It's amazing what people will do to make something like that go away. He's been helping me all along." He quirked a superior black eyebrow at her.

"Your scapegoat is in jail. There's no one left to blame if you kill me now."

"Thanks to you and Cruse, I have nothing left to lose. When Stanfield was arrested, the project fell through. Those bigwigs that pulled out, they can take a million-dollar hit and feel no pain. I lost *everything*. And they're all going to die, to pay for what they did to me. Every last one of them. But I'm starting with you. And Cruse."

He motioned again, wanting her to get in front of him. The phone—he'd see the phone. She took a hesitant step, but he grabbed her arm, jerking her forward, and she lost her grip on her one chance at getting help.

With every atom of her body resisting the movement, she wrestled past Slayton into the front room. He hauled her up against his hard angular body. His breath hot against her ear, he growled, "When we get outside, don't even make a single sound, or I swear, you're dead before you take another step."

Please, God, please help. She couldn't survive this on her own. She couldn't think of how to escape this predicament, but surely God had a plan.

Slayton dragged her toward the door. Training kicked in. She stomped down hard on the top of Slayton's foot. When he yelped, she jerked hard to the left and wrenched her arm free of his grasp.

The front door stood open. Close. She could make it. Almost there—a burning, searing pain cut across her calf muscle and she stumbled, falling hard in a heap on the floor. Did Slayton actually *shoot* her?

A split second later, Slayton yanked her off the floor to her feet. When she resisted, he grabbed her face, digging his fingers into the soft skin. The glassy, feverish expression in his once-friendly and familiar eyes goaded her into motion.

She punched her elbow into his ribs and tried to tug her arm loose from his iron grip. He slammed her back into the door frame. Pain ricocheted through her skull and blackness closed over her like a heavy blanket.

"Bayley!" Cruse took the steps up to her house three at a time, the dog racing up the steps beside him. His heart stuttered when he saw the door standing open. He pulled his weapon and swung into the house in one smooth motion. Clear.

He stepped cautiously to the bedroom door, and whipped

around the corner. Bedroom clear. Packing boxes sat out on the bed. The TV news was on, but muted. Dread hit him—clammy sweat popping out on his forehead. *Oh, Bayley, where did he take you?*

As he moved to the door, his foot tapped something that slid under the edge of the bed. He reached down and pulled out Bayley's cell phone. His heart sank even further.

A sharp bark from Scruffy, followed by a whine, drew Cruse out into the front room. The loyal dog stood in the kitchen by the door, standing over… *Oh, please, God, not blood.*

His first instinct was to head for the station. He needed backup. Big-time. Because every second that he lost looking for her, Bayley's life hung in the balance.

As he barreled into his Jeep, his eye fell on the file folder still in the passenger seat. La Plage. If he were Slayton, looking for revenge, or retribution, he'd go there. It was a guess. If he was wrong, he'd have wasted even more time. But he had to take a chance, because time, for Bayley, could be running out.

Cold seeped from the floor into Bayley's bones and dulled the sharp stinging pain in her head to a throb. In contrast, her leg screamed in protest to any tiny motion.

Where was she?

Slayton. Slayton had brought her here. Wherever here was. She slowly opened her eyes. And blinked. Dark. Terror rolled over her in a low, evil wave. Her arms and legs shook uncontrollably.

Bayley squeezed herself into a tight ball in the corner of the room, whimpering when she moved her leg. She could see nothing. Her hand right in front of her eyes—invisible in the blackness. Nobody knew where she was, nobody could help.

She didn't just *feel* alone, she *was*—utterly—alone. Her breath came in quick pants.

Slowly, Bayley eased her back up the wall, sliding her hands to the side to test the stretch of wall on either side of her. Nothing but more cold concrete. Reality loomed, and with it came a wave of despair that buckled her knees. She'd been shot, and she was trapped in a concrete cage. No help, no way out.

God, please.

Peace stole in where fear rampaged. Nothing had changed, yet everything had changed. *She wasn't alone.* God would never leave her. And she couldn't let fear get the best of her.

With her teeth, she made a small tear and ripped a band from around the bottom of her T-shirt. When she had it torn into one long strip, she wrapped it around her leg and tied it in a tight pressure bandage. Fighting through the pain, she drew in two deep breaths through her nose. She could not pass out again.

She'd find the door by moving along to her right. She slid along the wall, one step, then two, trying not to stumble. Her leg wouldn't hold her weight. She hit the ground hard, crying out as her wounded leg took the brunt of the fall. Bright colors swam in her vision.

I want to give up. I can't do this.

Yes, you can, came the answer back.

She pulled herself back to her feet and, with a weird leaning hop, made it to where she thought the door should be. Not daring to hope, she found the knob and turned it. Locked, of course.

Inch by painstaking inch, Bayley searched the wall for another exit, a vent, something, some way to escape this black pit. She fell to her knees, the gravel on the dirty floor digging into her skin. When she couldn't find the strength to stand again, she crawled. And her hand closed around something smooth and cold. She picked it up. A jagged edge caught her thumb.

She tore another piece off her T-shirt to wrap around her find. A piece of ragged sheet metal wasn't exactly a fierce weapon, but if Slayton came back, she wouldn't be defenseless.

She had no clue how long she'd been moving, but she had to rest. Dizziness assaulted her. With it came hopelessness as black as the room she was trapped in. How would anyone know where she was? How would anyone find her? Did anyone even know to look?

There was a very real possibility that she would die here. She didn't feel fear, or rage. But regret…if she didn't make it, she'd never get to tell Cruse how very deeply he was loved.

Dirt sprayed as Cruse slammed the brakes on the police-department SUV. He turned to Joe Sheehan. "We need to be ready for anything."

"Always." Joe flashed a grin. Every cop—shoot, probably every guy—loved heading into battle. It was how they were built.

Cruse usually relished the challenges of police work, but thoughts of Bayley consumed him. He wanted her safe, with him. Nothing else mattered. He'd changed. Or maybe just his perspective had changed. She'd made him want more for his life than just a job, just a badge.

All in. He knew now that though he'd dedicated his life to God, he hadn't trusted God enough to give his whole heart. He had to let go of everything he wanted, and hold on to what God had for him. It was time to fully trust God—for his life. And for Bayley's.

Cruse opened the back door of the SUV and Scruff jumped down. The construction site looked deserted. No workers in hard hats climbed, or suit-clad investors loitered. The breeze off the water blew the dusty surface of the site in meandering whirlwinds.

When Scruffy let out a bark and took off for the skeleton of the condominium building, Cruse and Joe were right behind him.

Cruse entered the building first, weapon drawn and ready. He whipped around as a gate to the stairs going down flapped and banged. No one there.

Scruff strained at his leash. Cruse motioned to Joe, *I'm going downstairs. Look around.*

In the center of the basement, Cruse could see the edges of what looked like a walled-in box surrounded by hallway. The dog pulled him toward it. Cruse circled the space in the hallway. Scruff sniffed at the door, sat down and whined.

Cruse let out a whistle to bring Joe and ran his light around the seam of the metal door. Tight as a drum. Cruse's stomach took a free fall as he reached the bottom of the door with the light. Shoved in the crack at the base of the door was what looked like plastic explosives. A ton of plastic explosives. In Cruse's limited experience, enough to implode the whole basement, maybe even the whole building.

A wire ran out of it into a grimy box. And beside the box was a single, shiny, black-looking blob. Cruse rubbed a finger across it and felt his chest squeeze painfully. Blood. Still wet, and almost certainly Bayley's.

The stairs cracked, and Cruse rolled into a motion as natural as breathing to him. When he realized it was Joe, he lowered his weapon and relaxed his stance. "I think Bayley's locked in this room, but the door's wired. We're going to need the bomb squad."

Joe's booted footsteps came closer, but Cruse didn't turn around again, his gaze glued to that lethal box. "And I think we're running out of time. Bayley's bleeding. She's hurt."

"All right. I'll go up to the truck and call for backup."

He started for the stairs, but turned back, compassion on his chiseled face. "Cruse. We're gonna get her out. We'll find a way."

Anguish speared through Cruse. If he'd been quicker, if he'd paid more attention, he could've prevented this. He'd let her down.

He placed a hand on the door. "Hey, honey. I don't know if you can hear me. Probably not. I know you're hurt, and scared, but I'm here. And I'm going to do everything in my power to get you out of there." He shifted on his feet, uneasy with the silence, unhappy with the lack of action, unused to having feelings cramming themselves in his throat.

He loved her so much.

He would do whatever it took to get her out. He would hold her in his arms again. "I'll get you out, baby," he whispered. "Or I'll die trying."

A patrol car and two fire trucks rolled in with the bomb squad, and the crime scene hummed with the workings of a well-oiled machine. What should have been reassuring to Cruse instead seemed an excruciatingly slow bureaucratic process.

He wanted to cut the wire, kick down the door and have Bayley in his arms. Now. Pacing the hallway, he watched the bomb squad set up, Slay's betrayal sitting heavy in his gut.

Cruse shook his head. *Slay's choice,* not Cruse's.

Cruse's cell phone rang. "Conyers," he snapped.

"Call off the bomb squad."

The hoarse whisper stopped Cruse midstep. "Slayton?"

"Bayley's dead if you don't call them off."

Cruse hesitated, thought it through. Slayton knew the protocol for a situation like this. He didn't have to have visual to know the call. "You're bluffing. You're nowhere near here."

"Are you going to risk her life on that assumption?"

Cruse took a deep breath. "Yes."

"How about a little demonstration to prove I'm telling the truth? Watch the foreman's trailer."

Cruse bolted up the stairs to the ground floor. And reached the top in time to see the foreman's trailer go up in a fireball of orange flame and black smoke. The concussion slammed Cruse into the plywood wall.

He blinked hard and shook his head to clear his vision. Out in the dirt parking lot, an officer was down. Two others crawled to him. Debris, flaming and otherwise, floated down around them.

Cruse screamed down the stairs to the men working on getting Bayley out. "Back off the box! *Back off the box!*"

Three of the bomb squad stormed up the stairs on their way out to the scene in the parking lot. Cruse hugged the wall to let them pass, and slammed his fist into the plywood barrier, not even wincing when the rough wood took the skin off his knuckles.

Sirens screamed in the distance. He held the cell phone back to his ear. "What do you want, Slayton?"

"That should be easy for you to figure out. I want you to suffer. You'll have to wait and watch knowing that every second that passes is one less second that Bayley has to live. How does it feel to know that I could blow her up right now?" He hesitated. "Or now!"

Slayton's cold laughter echoed in Cruse's brain, matching the cold knot in the pit of his stomach. *God, give me guidance, tell me the words to say.*

"Slayton, you're a good cop. Why are you doing this?"

Contempt oozed out of Slayton's voice. "Because, Cruse, I'm not a self-righteous jerk like you are. I don't want to be a cop forever. I was looking for a payoff and about to make it, too, if it hadn't been for those tree-hugging environmentalists."

"So you decided to take them out of the picture?"

"You can't even say it, can you, Cruse? I *killed* them. And if you had just backed off the case and let me handle it, you and your girlfriend would be fine."

And then Cruse knew. The pieces had been there from the beginning. He and Bayley had even commented on how distracted he had been by the stalker case; he just hadn't realized how right they had been. "You spent all that time and energy trying to divert my attention from the S.O.S case by pretending to be Bayley's stalker and you still couldn't succeed."

"If you'd focused on Bayley instead of S.O.S. like you were supposed to…if you hadn't been so diligent in requesting those files…things might be different. I want you to know, Cruse, how bad you messed up. It's your fault Bayley's in this mess."

Cruse remembered the feel of soft Bayley in his arms—so strong and so small. "Let her go. She's not part of this. Let her go and we'll take the kidnapping charge off the table."

"Whatever." Slay laughed. "As if I wouldn't be serving four life sentences for murder. Understand this. There will be no deal, no negotiation. If I go down, I'm taking you with me." Desperation tinged his voice. "I've got *nothing* to lose."

FOURTEEN

The connection went dead in Cruse's hand. He looked at his fingers, clenched white around the tiny phone.

"Stand down," he said to the bomb squad tech. "For now."

He turned around, looking for Scruff in the darkness of the basement. The temporary lights they'd brought in cast obscene shadows on the walls. Giving a low whistle, he called the dog.

Outside, Joe held his cell phone to his ear, pacing the parking lot as Cruse rounded the top of the stairs. When Cruse caught his eye, he crossed to meet him.

"What did you find out?"

"It's not good," the younger officer said. "I talked to Slayton's landlord. He took care of his mother, who lived in the rental house with him, until about two months ago when she got too sick. She's been in the hospital since then. She died two days ago waiting on a heart."

"Slayton was counting on the money from his investments to pay the hospital bills."

"Yeah, it looks that way. I talked to Mr. Stanfield, too. The investment group went belly-up. Slayton's pretty much got nothing left to lose."

That was what Cruse was afraid of. Nothing left to bargain with meant no negotiation would work. Slayton's life would be the only chip, and it was worthless, because he didn't care if he lived or not. He just wanted to take with him as many of the people he thought had wronged him as possible.

He clenched his teeth. "We can't get to the bomb. Slayton's threatening to blow it if we even get close."

Joe picked up his mirrored sunglasses, scratched the slick, shaved dome of his head, and settled the glasses back in place, frustration beginning to visibly eat at him as well. "All right. Tell me everything you know about this place."

Cruse thought, trying to remember what he'd found out from the Stanfields. "The basement's partially finished, along with the vault, the laundry room, the ductwork." He met Joe's eyes, and saw the light dawn.

"The ductwork." They said it together.

"If she's in the laundry room—and I think she is—there's a laundry chute, right?" With the idea, Cruse felt a slight lightening of the weight on his chest. Just maybe, they had a shot at getting her out.

Cruse started toward the police department's SUV, with Joe at his heels. He pulled binoculars out of the truck and began scanning the incomplete structure in front of him. After a moment, he handed the binoculars to the junior officer. "Look to the left of the center of the building. There's a silver box that looks like it goes all the way down. It's wider than the rest of the ductwork."

"That's got to be it." Joe brought the glasses down from his face, wrapped the cord around them and handed them back to Cruse. "Now the question is, how do we do it without him noticing?"

"We need a distraction." Cruse opened the back of the SUV and pulled out the tactical equipment and rappelling gear. "Enough of one to get us up to about the third or fourth floor. If he can see in the basement, he's low enough that maybe he can't see up there."

"And if he can?"

"Then we're toast." Cruse laughed humorlessly as he strapped on his Kevlar vest and handed Joe the other one. "But if we can't find him and we can't get her out, then we're toast anyway."

Joe pulled out another coil of thick rope.

Cruse stopped him with a hand on his chest. "You don't have to be up there. There's a chance, maybe a good chance, that he'll see me and blow the building."

"You're going to need me to haul your butt out of the basement if...*when* you find Bayley. I've got your back, sir." He met Cruse's eyes. "And, Cruse—I'm praying."

Cruse felt his eyes fill. His voice came out hoarse with emotion. And all he could say was, "Thanks."

He slung a coil of rope and his harness over his shoulder and adjusted his lip mic. Full-out determination and focus were a necessary part of this mission. For years, Cruse had borne the weight of guilt that he'd let his sister down when he'd gotten distracted. No distraction would alter his course today. God was in control, and the bad guy wasn't going to win this one.

Joe's grin flashed again in the darkness. "Assuming all goes well, we'll need another distraction to get out of the building. Do you think those bomb squad guys know how to set them as well as they defuse them?"

Antsy and ready to move, Cruse and Joe, along with a firefighter with high-angle rescue experience, waited in the shadow of the building. Their plan was as perfect as they could make it. On cue, at 8:20, explosion number one kicked off. Cruse, Joe and the firefighter advanced silently up four sets of plywood steps.

Ninety seconds to get in place before explosion number two. As they hit the top of the stairs, the firefighter had the block gun ready, so the sound of the second explosion would mask him setting the block in the concrete pillar. The second block would be set in a beam above them—during explosion number three. The pulley system they rigged in the blocks would allow them to drop Cruse and pull the two of them up smoothly, quickly and quietly.

Cruse stepped into the rescue harness. Joe hooked the ropes through Cruse's harness and tied them off.

As Cruse peered through the square cut into the laundry chute where eventually maids would have dropped dirty linens, utter blackness reached up and wrapped around him. Drawing in a deep breath, he tried to ignore the feeling of panic that began in his belly and made his arms tingle. He would get Bayley out. *He would.*

Cruse climbed in and gave a thumbs-up, giving them the go-ahead to ease him down into the inky depths. The plan was for him to drop about a floor at a time, rest and drop again. But there would be nothing for him to hold on to, nothing solid to put his feet on. Nothing but black space.

At the first stop, Cruse tried to get his bearings. The absolute darkness felt like a solid mass encroaching on him from every angle. He could only move each elbow inches before he touched the metal walls of the chute. He swung a little, torquing in the narrow space. His breath hissed as his subconscious began to tell him he was in trouble.

He tried to counteract it with reality. *You're not in a closet. You're not four years old, or six. You're a grown man. A cop. You're doing a job.*

Joe's muted voice in his ear grounded him. "Hang tight, man. You're doing great."

If God is for me, who can be against me? Cruse's gloved fingers closed around the rope and his breath eased as they dropped him another floor. This time when the blackness began to try to suffocate him, he rehearsed what he would do when he got to Bayley. But the dark was stronger. It closed in on him, pressing on his chest.

I can't do this. Yes, he could. He could beat this for Bayley.

The rope jerked and he dropped a foot and halted for a long second before they eased him down one more floor. He listened, forcing himself to concentrate. He should be getting close to the basement now. Maybe he was at the first floor?

In the absence of sight, his hearing seemed more acute, the creaks and cracks of the building and even the odd voice from outside loud in the metal confines of the chute. Then he heard it. The familiar tapping of fingers against metal. It wouldn't be Bayley in the basement, not tapping that rhythm. He knew exactly what that tapping meant.

"Joe," he breathed in the lip mic. "Slayton's in the air-conditioning ductwork."

"Roger that," came Joe's cool voice. "Watch your back."

Cruse began to drop again, but the rope snagged on something, something up high, at or near the top. His breath caught as the harness jerked him up—hard. He dangled, spinning in the freakish darkness, and panic began to claw its way to the surface. He threw his head back to avoid his mother's foot as she kicked at him. *"Get back in that closet, you miserable brat."*

He sucked a breath in as her slap caught him across the face. *"All you do is eat my food, and take up space. I wish you'd never been born."*

His chest burned for oxygen, his breaths sharp and shallow. *No.*

He shook his head. That was in the past. It wasn't about that little boy anymore. He knew that he was a new person, a new creature in Christ. He'd been made in the image of God and he was worthy of being born because of that simple fact alone.

Unbidden, images of Bayley came to his mind—playing

with the dog, waiting tables at Sip This, her unbridled generosity. And Sailor, always steadfast. His friends at the department.

All people he loved. All people who—right or wrong, deserved or not—loved him in return. Sailor didn't hold him responsible for what happened to her. And by holding that pain close, by keeping it in the forefront, it was a constant reminder to her.

He didn't think any less of her for what happened to her. Why would he punish himself for coming from the same background?

God, through the sacrifice of Jesus Christ, had forgiven him of his sins. Cruse just hadn't been able to forgive himself. He'd hadn't been able to see what was in front of his face. When he got out of here, he was making some changes. His life wasn't about the past. It was about the present, starting *right now.*

The rope came loose and Cruse started down again with a jolt. Joe's voice in his ear, "Sorry about that. We hit a snag."

No kidding.

At the base of the chute, he still couldn't see, but the air felt cooler and when the chute ended, he felt space open up around him. He could take a deep breath, feeling his lungs fill with oxygen. His boots touched concrete floor, and solid ground had never felt so good.

"Down."

He reached into his pocket and drew out his penlight. Clicking it on, he ran it over the surface of the wall in front of him. The door was there. Cruse turned slowly to the right, panning the light over each surface. He didn't see anything.

Starting back at the door, he moved the light to the left, again searching each inch of the wall and floor with his light. And saw nothing but some old barrels of what looked like sheetrock mud.

Despair rocketed through Cruse, weakening his knees. They'd been wrong and Slayton had been playing them all along.

A soft, barely audible sigh sounded from the other side of the room. Cruse scanned with the light again, this time seeing what his flashlight had missed. A bare foot—dusty enough to blend in with the concrete floor—stuck out from behind the barrels. Bayley!

Cruse rushed to her. She lay on her side, a crude, blood-soaked bandage tied around her leg. *Oh, Bay.*

He threw his glove off and reached two fingers out to her neck. Her pulse was weak, but steady.

Thank You, God.

Her quick indrawn breath startled Cruse. In the diffuse light of the tiny flashlight, her eyes were wide and terrified. She drew back from him, brandishing a piece of metal in her hand.

"Bayley, it's me," he whispered. She whimpered and pressed herself even farther back into the corner. Not able to talk out loud to ease her fear, he did the only thing he knew to do. He pulled her into his arms. She fought him, pushing away, lashing out with the makeshift weapon. He smothered a grunt of pain as she caught him across the arm, but didn't let go.

He pulled her tight into his chest and spoke into her ear. "Baby, it's Cruse. I'm here to help you. I'm not going to let you get hurt anymore."

Her whole body went limp and for a moment he thought she'd passed out again, but he felt her tears like rain on his shirt, and her trembling.

In his earpiece, Joe whispered, "Sir, I hate to hurry you, but we've got six minutes. Can Bayley make it up the rope?"

"She will."

He sat Bayley back and looked in her eyes, the flashlight

barely providing enough light. He didn't know how much blood she'd lost. Or how much longer she could hold on. His heart stumbled. He needed to hurry.

"Bay, listen. I'm going to put you in a harness and get you out of here. Joe's waiting at the top for you, okay?"

She nodded weakly as he unhooked her harness from his waist and began to put it around her. "This is important, Bayley. You have to stay awake. You got it? You've done so good, babe. Hang in there for this one more thing."

He carried her to the ropes dangling out of the laundry chute and tied her into the harness, placing her hands on the ropes and showing her how to hold on.

Because he needed to, he touched his lips to hers in a brief, gentle caress. "I love you, Bayley. Stay awake."

Into the lip mic, he said, "Take her up."

Awareness came in fits and starts to Bayley. The whirlwind of activity that began when Cruse found her hadn't backed off. It was a maelstrom of sound, light and voices.

She joggled and bounced, dreaming of Joe Sheehan pulling her out of some kind of tube. Her confused mind tried to make sense of the chaos, but sleep seemed to stalk her like a mother after a child, very insistent that she should rest. She should go along, she thought, because she had never been quite so tired.

"Ouch!" She opened her eyes to see the inside of a white box, and people she didn't know stabbing her with needles. "Get off me!"

One of the strangers backed off and opened a door—she could hear it open—and called, "Cruse?"

Good. Cruse would set them straight. He wouldn't let some weirdo with a needle go poking at her. His worried face appeared above her. She beamed at him, her champion knight. "Hey, Cruse. I missed you."

His smile wobbled. "I missed you, too, Bay."

"Cruse, you gotta tell these people to get away from me." She dropped her voice to a whisper. "You might need your gun."

Amusement laced his voice. "I don't think I'll need my gun, sugar. You need to let Starla and Daniel do their jobs. They're here to help you, I promise."

That wasn't what Cruse was supposed to say. She scowled.

He looked up and caught the eye of one of *those* people.

The man—paramedic?—said, "The round went straight through. She's lost a lot of blood, but…she was lucky."

"Cruse…"

His cell phone rang, interrupting her thoughts. He stepped out of her line of sight. She drifted, hearing Cruse's voice, hard and scary sounding. "You do whatever you have to, Slayton. You're coming out of there one way or another. In handcuffs, or a body bag."

So it wasn't over yet. Bayley reared up, but those pesky people with the needles pushed her back again. She listened intently for Cruse's next words.

Then he said, "I believe you would blow her up, Slayton. But that's an empty threat. *Because I got her out.*"

Bayley heard a roar, like a faraway bear, and then she had to close her eyes because there was a really loud explosion— the loudest she'd ever heard.

Cruse threw himself on top of her and the paramedics did, too. The ambulance shuddered and shook as things rained down on the roof from the building where she'd been held. The black horror of what could have happened to her crept into the corner of her mind.

But it didn't happen because Cruse had been there and gotten her out. God protected them, gave them a future.

Cruse was so heavy on her that she couldn't breathe almost, but she didn't mind, because Cruse felt so strong that she didn't want to worry anymore.

* * *

Cruse pulled into his driveway four days later with Bayley in the seat beside him. She'd agreed to come to his house with no argument. He still wasn't sure how that happened. At the moment she wasn't saying a word. Her mouth was too busy hanging open.

"Lime green, Cruse? You painted your entire house *lime green?*" Her voice—which she'd obviously found—ended on a squeak. "Why?"

"It's not boring."

She laughed, the full throaty chuckle that he loved. "No, it's certainly not that. And I wanted you to finish painting your house. I just never imagined you'd be so daring. I love it."

He opened the passenger door of his Jeep and swung her into his arms. "I figured it was fitting since life with you will never be boring."

He turned the corner from the stairs onto the deck, careful not to jar her leg where she'd had surgery. Her muffled gasp told him she'd seen his next surprise. "Oh, Cruse."

She sniffled a little and he narrowed his eyes at her. "You're not going to cry, are you?"

"I don't know, maybe. It's so sweet. You're going to teach me to surf?"

He grinned and flipped his too-long hair off his forehead. "Just as soon as your leg is healed." He nodded at the bright-yellow surfboard that he'd leaned next to his by the front door to his house. "It's top-of-the-line and should be super-easy to learn on."

"It's perfect, Cruse. You couldn't have bought me anything better."

The diamond burning a hole in his pocket ought to top the surfboard. At least he hoped it would. He had a knot in his stomach the size of Mount Saint Helens. What if she didn't want to get married? She really did like being independent.

Maybe she wanted a few years to be on her own. If she did, he'd just have to suck it up and wait for God's timing. He'd discovered he was a one-woman man. He could wait.

When he'd kicked open the door—very manly move that, he hoped she was impressed—he asked her, "Couch or chair?"

"Couch."

He set her on his oversize couch and piled pillows around her. "Are you all right?"

"Yes. Now sit down. I'm tired of being fussed over."

He eased down behind her, careful not to jostle her.

"Cruse, seriously. I'm fine, but you're worrying me."

"I'm fine. I'm great. Really." Except for the nerves doing the shimmy in his stomach. The past few days had been hard, but Jake had helped him accept that Slayton's choices had led to his death. While Cruse would always regret that he couldn't help his friend, he couldn't hold himself responsible for another person's actions.

"Thanks for taking me to see Thomas before we came home."

"There's still some evidence to sort through, but it looks pretty clear that Slayton was behind the killings and stalking. Thomas went along because Slayton blackmailed him. There will still be charges, but it won't be nearly as bad as we thought." He picked up her hand, laced his fingers through hers. "You were right about him all along. We should all have someone believe in us that much."

"Cruse—"

"No, let me, Bayley. I learned something while you were being held. I'm not afraid of the past anymore. What scares the daylights out of me is the idea of a future without you in it."

He dug in his pocket and came out with the ring box, the corner of his mouth hitching up when he heard Bayley's involuntary gasp.

The ring, a fiery one-carat diamond solitaire, reminded him of Bayley. He so wanted to see it on her finger, to hear her say that she'd belong to him.

He cleared his throat, his eyes stinging. "I used to dream of having a real family when I was a kid, but I never thought it would happen to me. I love you, Bayley Foster."

"I love you, too," Bayley whispered. "And nothing you do or say could make me change my mind."

"I know." And the wonder of that still stunned him. Pulling her up snug against his side, he turned her so they could see the sun, beginning to sink over the Gulf of Mexico, a bright orange ball of fire. "Bayley, I want to watch sunsets with you, drink coffee on the deck, surf as the dawn is breaking, watch our kids play in the sand…I want it all. But I only want it with you."

"Are you sure?"

She was so stubborn. "I painted my house lime green. Yes, I'm sure. I want to marry you."

She twisted around to face him, her eyes meeting his in a long, loving caress. She held out her left hand. "Yes. Yes, I'll marry you." She sniffed back tears. "We'll ride off into the sunset together."

Cruse glanced back at the sun, hot, liquid red dipping into the ocean, and gripped her hand, sliding the ring into its place on her finger.

"Nah, we'll paddle into the sunset on our surfboards."

* * * * *

Dear Reader,

After being attacked and very nearly killed, Bayley *savors* the life God has blessed her with. She doesn't want to need anyone, but Bayley has to learn to trust God for every need, even when the answer comes in a very unexpected way.

Cruse helps Bayley face her fears, but it's when he faces losing her that Cruse realizes the truth: while he's given his life to God, he's never truly learned to trust enough in God's forgiving grace to give his whole heart.

Sometimes trusting in God in a challenging situation is the most difficult thing we can do. After all, we can't *see* Him. In *Perfect Target,* both Bayley and Cruse are afraid of what the future holds because of an uncertain present, but both find God to be trustworthy in the most taxing of situations.

You may not have been stalked and kidnapped, but I'm willing to bet that you've faced some pretty challenging situations in your life. If you've ever had a toddler, you know what I mean! I pray that you seek God and find Him faithful, not only in the big things in life, but in everyday small things, too.

All God's best,

Stephanie Newton

DISCUSSION QUESTIONS

1. What led Bayley to open Hope House? How did she help the women there face their future?

2. Cruse, as a new Christian, finds himself faced with temptations and situations that are difficult to overcome. He is successful, but only through God's power. What are some things that tempt you to fall into old behaviors, or new situations that might be dangerous? What empowers you to overcome them?

3. Bayley faces a life of expectations. She chooses to go her own way, following a life that she feels God led her to. Do you think it is hurtful for Bayley that her parents don't understand her? Is it difficult for you to do what God wants, rather than what others expect of you? Why or why not?

4. In Cruse's past, he faced alcoholism and poverty. He overcame those things in his life, but the wounds of his past hadn't fully healed. What were the most important things God taught Cruse before he could completely be free of his past?

5. In *Perfect Target,* Bayley bought paintbrushes, redecorated her house, insisted on staying alone, and fixed her faucet with instructions from the Internet. Why was it so important to Bayley that she learn to be independent?

6. Bayley believed that Cruse would be just like every other protector that she'd ever been around. As she got to know him, she found that he was different in many ways. What

causes us to stereotype and how can we overcome those stereotypes?

7. After a life of feeling different, Bayley found it difficult to believe that anyone would want to be her friend. What did she find through her church that she'd always been looking for?

8. Cruse believed he had failed his sister. Why did he have such a hard time accepting forgiveness—from his sister and from God?

9. As the stalker targets Bayley, she finds it harder to trust God. Have you ever experienced a time when, like Bayley, you didn't see God's hand? What made you realize that God can be trusted?

10. Cruse buys Bayley a dog so that she can stay in her home. Why is that gift so meaningful for Bayley? Has anyone ever given you the perfect gift? Explain.

11. Bayley gives Cruse a gift, also: the gift of being seen through nonjudgmental eyes. Why did that mean so much to Cruse? What would it mean to you, to have that kind of loyalty?

12. When Cruse realized who the stalker was, he believed that he might have let Bayley down. Why did Cruse feel responsible for everyone's safety? Have you ever felt accountable for something that wasn't really up to you?

13. Bayley learns that love doesn't mean losing yourself, it means learning to be dependent on a God who loves you, and learning to count on other people who care

about you. How do we push others away in our bid for independence and autonomy? How can we draw them closer as a part of the family of God?

14. Cruse learned that love is worth taking a risk for. How did he take that leap of faith? Is there something that you're afraid of that will take a leap of faith to overcome?

*Turn the page for a sneak preview of
bestselling author
Jillian Hart's novella
"Finally a Family."*

*One of two heartwarming stories
celebrating motherhood in
IN A MOTHER'S ARMS.*

*On sale April 2009, only from
Steeple Hill Love Inspired Historical.*

Chapter One

Montana Territory, 1884

Molly McKaslin sat in her rocking chair in her cozy little shanty with her favorite book in hand. The lush new-spring green of the Montana prairie spread out before her like a painting, framed by the wooden window. The blue sky was without a single cloud to mar it. Lemony sunshine spilled over the land and across the open window's sill. The door was wedged open, letting the outside noises in—the snap of laundry on the clothesline and the chomping crunch of an animal grazing. My, it sounded terribly close.

The peaceful afternoon quiet shattered with a crash. She leaped to her feet to see her good—and only—china vase splintered on the newly washed wood floor. She stared in shock at the culprit standing at her other window. A golden cow with a white blaze down her face poked her head farther across the sill. The bovine gave a woeful moo. One look told her this was the only animal in the yard.

"And just what are you doing out on your own?" She set her book aside.

The cow lowed again. She was a small heifer, still probably more baby than adult. The cow lunged against the sill, straining toward the cookie racks on the table.

"At least I know how to catch you." She grabbed a cookie off the rack and the heifer's eyes widened. "I don't recognize you, so I don't think you belong here."

Molly skirted around the mess on the floor and headed toward the door. This was the consequence of agreeing to live in the country, when she had vowed never to do so again. But her path had led her to this opportunity, living on her cousin's land and helping the family. God had quite a sense of humor, indeed.

Before she could take two steps into the soft, lush grass surrounding her shanty, the cow came running, head down, big brown eyes fastened on the cookie. The ground shook.

Uh-oh. Molly's heart skipped two beats.

"No, Sukie, no!" High, girlish voices carried on the wind.

Molly briefly caught sight of two identical school-aged girls racing down the long dirt road. The animal was too single-minded to respond. She pounded the final few yards, her gaze fixed on the cookie.

"Stop, Sukie. Whoa." Molly kept her voice low and kindly firm. She knew cows responded to kindness better than to anything else. She also knew they were not good at stopping, so she dropped the cookie on the ground and neatly stepped out of the way. The cow skidded well past the cookie and the place where Molly had been standing.

"It's right here." She showed the cow where the oatmeal treat was resting in the clean grass. While the animal backed up and nipped up the goody, Molly grabbed the cow's rope halter.

"Good. She didn't stomp you into bits," one of the girls said in serious relief. "She ran me over real good just last week."

"We thought you were a goner," the second girl said. "She's real nice, but she doesn't see very well."

"She sees well enough to have found me." Molly studied the girls. They both had identical black braids and golden-hazel eyes and fine-boned porcelain faces. One twin wore a green calico dress with matching sunbonnet, while the other wore blue. She recognized the girls from church and around town. "Aren't you the doctor's children?"

"Yep, that's us." The first girl offered a beaming, dimpled smile. "I'm Penelope and that's Prudence. We're real glad you found Sukie."

"We wouldn't want a cougar to get her."

"Or a bear."

What adorable children. A faint scattering of freckles dappled across their sun-kissed noses, and there was glint of trouble in their eyes as the twins looked at one another. The place in her soul thirsty for a child of her own ached painfully. She felt hollow and empty, as if her body would always remember carrying the baby she had lost. For one moment it was as if the wind died and the earth vanished.

"Hey, what is she eating?" One of the girls tumbled forward. "It smells like a cookie. You are a bad girl, Sukie."

"Did she walk into your house and eat off the counter?" Penelope wanted to know.

The grass crinkled beneath her feet as the cow tugged her toward the girls. "No, she went through the window."

Penelope went up on tiptoe. "I see them. They look real good."

Molly gazed down at their sweet and innocent faces. She wasn't fooled. Then again, she was a soft touch. "I'll see what I can do."

She headed back inside. "Do you girls need help getting the cow home?"

"No. She's real tame." Penelope and the cow trailed after her, hesitating outside the door. "We can lead her anywhere."

"Yeah, she only runs off when she's looking for us."

"Thank you so much, Mrs.—" Penelope took the napkin-wrapped stack of cookies. "We don't know your name."

"This is the McKaslin ranch," Prudence said thoughtfully. "But I know you're not Mrs. McKaslin."

"I'm the cousin. I moved here this last winter. You can call me Molly."

Penelope gave her twin a cookie. Beneath the brim of her sunbonnet, her face crinkled with serious thought. "You don't know our pa yet?"

"No, I only know Dr. Frost by reputation. I hear he's a fine doctor." That was all she knew. Of course she had seen his fancy black buggy speeding down the country roads at all hours. Sometimes she caught a brief sight of the man driving as the horse-drawn vehicle passed—an impression of a black Stetson, a strong granite profile and impressively wide shoulders.

Although she was on her own and free to marry, she paid little heed to eligible men. All she knew of Dr. Sam Frost was that he was a widower and a father and a faithful man, for he often appeared very serious in church. She reached through the open door to where her coats hung on wall pegs and worked the sash off her winter wool.

Prudence smiled. "Our pa's real nice and you make good cookies."

"And you're real pretty." Penelope was so excited she didn't notice Sukie stealing her cookie. "Do you like Pa?"

"I don't know the man, so I can't like him. I suppose I can't dislike him either." She bent to secure the sash around Sukie's halter. "Let me walk you girls across the road."

"You ought to come home with us." Penelope grinned. "Then you can meet Pa."

"Do you want to get married?" Penelope's feet were planted.

So were Prudence's. "Yes! You could marry Pa. Do you want to?"

"M-marry your pa?" Shock splashed over her like icy water.

"Sure. You could be our ma."

"And then Pa wouldn't be so lonely anymore."

Molly blinked. The words were starting to sink in. The poor girls, wishing so much for a mother that they would take any stranger who was kind to them. "No, I certainly cannot marry a perfect stranger, but thank you for asking. I would take you two in a heartbeat."

"You would?" Penelope looked surprised. "Really?"

"We're an awful lot of trouble. Our housekeeper said that three times today since church."

"Does your pa know you propose on his behalf?"

"Now he does," a deep baritone answered. Dr. Frost marched into sight, rounding the corner of the shanty. His hat brim shaded his face, casting shadows across his chiseled features, giving him an even more imposing appearance. "Girls! Home! Not another word."

"But we had to save Sukie."

"She could have been eaten by a wolf."

Molly watched the good doctor's mouth twitch. She couldn't be sure, but a flash of humor could have twinkled in the depths of his eyes.

"You must be the cousin." He swept off his hat. The twinkle faded from his eyes and the hint of a grin from his lips. It was clear that while his daughters amused him, she did not. "I had no idea you would be so young."

"And pretty," Penelope, obviously the troublemaker, added mischievously.

Molly's face heated. The poor girl must need glasses. Although Molly was still young, time and sadness had made its mark on her. The imposing man had turned into granite as he faced her. Of course he had overheard his daughters' proposal, so that might explain it.

She smiled and took a step away from him. "Dr. Frost, I'm

glad you found your daughters. I was about ready to bring them back to you."

"I'll save you the trouble." He didn't look happy. "Girls, take that cow home. I need to stay and apologize to Miss McKaslin."

She was a "Mrs." but she didn't correct him. She had put away her black dresses and her grief. Her marriage had mostly been a long string of broken dreams. She did better when she didn't remember. "Please don't be too hard on the girls on my behalf. Sukie's arrival livened up my day."

"At least there was no harm done." He winced. "There was harm? What happened?"

"I didn't say a word."

"No, but I could see it on your face."

Had he been watching her so closely? Or had she been so unguarded? Perhaps it was his closeness. She could see bronze flecks in his gold eyes, and smell the scents of soap and spring clinging to his shirt. A spark of awareness snapped within her like a candle newly lit. "It was a vase. Sukie knocked it off my windowsill when she tried to eat the flowers, but it was an accident."

"The girls should take better care of their pet." He drew his broad shoulders into an unyielding line. He turned to check on the twins, who were progressing down the road. The wind ruffled his dark hair. He seemed distant. Lost. "How much was the vase worth?"

How did she tell him it was without price? Perhaps it would be best not to open that door to her heart. "It was simply a vase."

"No, it was more." He stared at his hat clutched in both hands. "Was it a gift?"

"No, it was my mother's."

"And is she gone?"

"Yes."

"Then I cannot pay you its true value. I'm sorry." His gaze met hers with startling intimacy. Perhaps a door was open to his heart as well, because sadness tilted his eyes. He looked like a man with many regrets.

She knew well the weight of that burden. "Please, don't worry about it."

"The girls will replace it." His tone brooked no argument, but it wasn't harsh. "About what my daughters said to you."

"Do you mean their proposal? Don't worry. It's plain to see they are simply children longing for a mother's love."

"Thank you for understanding. Not many folks do."

"Maybe it's because I know something about longing. Life never turns out the way you plan it."

"No. Life can hand you more sorrow than you can carry." Although he did not move a muscle, he appeared changed. Stronger, somehow. Greater. "I'm sorry the girls troubled you, Miss McKaslin."

Mrs., but again she didn't correct him. It was the sorrow she carried that stopped her from it. She preferred to stand in the present with sunlight on her face. "It was a pleasure, Dr. Frost. What blessings you have in those girls."

"That I know." He tipped his hat to her, perhaps a nod of respect, and left her alone with the restless wind and the door still open in her heart.

* * * * *

REQUEST YOUR FREE BOOKS!

2 FREE RIVETING INSPIRATIONAL NOVELS PLUS 2 FREE MYSTERY GIFTS

Love Inspired.
SUSPENSE

YES! Please send me 2 FREE Love Inspired® Suspense novels and my 2 FREE mystery gifts (gifts are worth about $10). After receiving them, if I don't wish to receive any more books, I can return the shipping statement marked "cancel". If I don't cancel, I will receive 4 brand-new novels every month and be billed just $4.24 per book in the U.S. or $4.74 per book in Canada, plus 25¢ shipping and handling per book and applicable taxes, if any*. That's a savings of over 20% off the cover price! I understand that accepting the 2 free books and gifts places me under no obligation to buy anything. I can always return a shipment and cancel at any time. Even if I never buy another book, the two free books and gifts are mine to keep forever.

123 IDN ERXX 323 IDN ERXM

Name	(PLEASE PRINT)

Address		Apt. #

City	State/Prov.	Zip/Postal Code

Signature (if under 18, a parent or guardian must sign)

Order online at www.LoveInspiredSuspense.com
Or mail to Steeple Hill Reader Service:

IN U.S.A.: P.O. Box 1867, Buffalo, NY 14240-1867
IN CANADA: P.O. Box 609, Fort Erie, Ontario L2A 5X3

Not valid to current subscribers of Love Inspired Suspense books.

Want to try two free books from another series?
Call 1-800-873-8635 or visit www.morefreebooks.com

* Terms and prices subject to change without notice. N.Y. residents add applicable sales tax. Canadian residents will be charged applicable provincial taxes and GST. Offer not valid in Quebec. This offer is limited to one order per household. All orders subject to approval. Credit or debit balances in a customer's account(s) may be offset by any other outstanding balance owed by or to the customer. Please allow 4 to 6 weeks for delivery. Offer available while quantities last.

Your Privacy: Steeple Hill Books is committed to protecting your privacy. Our Privacy Policy is available online at www.SteepleHill.com or upon request from the Reader Service. From time to time we make our lists of customers available to reputable third parties who may have a product or service of interest to you. If you would prefer we not share your name and address, please check here. ☐

LISUS08R

Love Inspired
SUSPENSE

TITLES AVAILABLE NEXT MONTH

On sale April 14, 2009

CODE OF HONOR by Lenora Worth
Get in, save the girl and get back out. CHAIM agent
Brice Whelan's agenda seems foolproof...until he tries
to rescue missionary/nurse Selena Carter. When danger
follows Selena home, Brice has to protect her, which means
sticking by her side—whether she wants him there or not.

CLOUD OF SUSPICION by Patricia Davids
Without a Trace
Leather-jacketed rebel Patrick Rivers has always had a
bad reputation. And now that he's back in town to settle
his stepfather's estate, Patrick knows he isn't welcome.
But the chance to keep Shelby Mason safe could be reason
enough to stay.

MURDER AT EAGLE SUMMIT by Virginia Smith
A body found on the slopes turns the wedding guests at
Eagle Summit ski resort into suspects. Liz Carmichael might
be a witness, so she files a police report...with her ex-fiancé,
Deputy Tim Richards. After three years apart, she can
finally make things right—unless the killer finds her first.

SHADOWS ON THE RIVER by Linda Hall
Ally Roarke was fourteen when she witnessed a murder...
and was forced out of town by the teenage killer's
prominent parents. Years later, the killer is a respected
businessman. And Ally, now a single mom, can't let the past
go. Especially when there's another death close to home.